THE SILVER DESOTO

PATTY LOU FLOYD

COUNCIL OAK BOOKS/TULSA

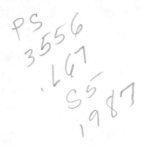

Council Oak Books
1428 South St. Louis
Tulsa, Oklahoma 74120
800/247-8850
918/587-6454 in Oklahoma

Manufactured in the United States of America.

First Edition.

Library of Congress Catalog Number 86-072491
ISBN 0-933031-03-3

Stamping and embossing of cover illustration by Fine Arts Engraving

BOOK AND COVER DESIGN BY CAROL HARALSON

*To those who gave me the heart to try.
With special thanks to Paul Scott, who showed me the way in,
to Winston Weathers, who showed me ways out,
and to my writers' group, who gave me the will to keep going.*

CONTENTS

SECRETS

AM SITTING AT the breakfast room table, writing the Farewell Speech for my high-school graduation, when I hear it — the screen door out on the back porch, rattling in its frame.

And I'm afraid.

It can't be Richard . . . this is Tuesday. Richard doesn't mow the yard until Thursday.

Again the rattling.

Telling myself there's nothing *outside* to be afraid of, I get up and head through the kitchen, over to the look-through window in the kitchen door.

Squinting down the length of the screened back porch, a tunnel of shade that runs between the house on one side and a thicket of mulberry trees on the other, I can see only a blinding rectangle of sunlight at the opposite end, and in it — as though giant scissors had cut out a patch of the light — a squat silhouette.

Not Richard — Richard is tall and spidery.

Telling myself again there is nothing outside the house to fear, I open the kitchen door and step out onto the back porch. Blinking against the sunlight at the far door, I can see now that, whoever it is waiting for me there, it is a woman. A black woman. Certainly a common enough sight at the back doors of Dixter . . . but not at ours.

For we never keep help. Except when someone in the family is dying.

"Miss Betty don' 'member me," the woman says, her voice filtering through the wheeze of labored, asthmatic breathing.

"Ethel!" Though her face is still in shadow, the sound of that long reach for air has triggered memory and recognition.

"Miss Betty do 'member," she grins.

I can see her features now, the plaits of hair thinner than when I last saw her, the front teeth longer, hanging looser in the gums.

"Come in, Ethel," I say, opening the screen door.

She sidles in, circles me at arm's length, studying me shyly out of the sides of her eyes, her head lowered. "You a young lady," she concludes.

4

"Next month I graduate," I answer.

"Then you be leavin' us, I spec?"

"For college . . ." I catch myself, "that is, if Nanna's well enough."

"I heerd about yer grammaw," she says, looking at the rows of Nanna's canning jars along the side of the porch. Then, still not looking me in the eye, she adds, "I be sayin' to mysef, 'Ethel, Miss Betty could mos' likely be usin' some hep'.'"

Facing away now from the glare of the door, back into the dimness of the porch, I can see Ethel's dark face clearly, shade upon shade, memory upon memory, and I know I have opened the door to the full face of my fears: *Nanna is going to die.*

And Ethel has come to help me. She who knows that only in last illnesses do we keep help.

Always, in those illnesses, it has been Ethel who has come to us, unbidden, out of whatever life she lives, who has stayed with us through the last days, through the funeral, for however long it took for the household to get "straightened 'round," until the day Nanna would send her away, to return to that other life.

The first was my aunt's. My mother's younger sister.

"Little Auntie" I called her.

I was four years old. Little Auntie was twenty-five. Mother, twenty-seven.

Little Auntie looked just like those sultry-eyed movie stars whose pictures, right alongside Rudloph Valentino's, lined the foyer of the Palace, Dixter's movie theatre. The Palace, in its way and in its day, was as central to Dixter life as the First Baptist Church: one brought another world to us; the other spoke of a world where we could go. Both to the movies and to the church, men and women wore their best.

At the church they were greeted by the pastor, acting like he owned it; at the Palace, by Uncle Ted and Little Auntie, who *did* own it. Each night Uncle Ted stood in the foyer taking tickets — dressed, they said, like the Prince of Wales, in knickers and bow tie; while Little Auntie sat in the box office, taking money — dressed as nearly like the stars lining the walls of the foyer as Dixter's customs and Nanna's sewing machine would allow (the sewing machine that, for years, had helped support the family).

Knowing that under her Theda Bara get-up lay the heart of a prairie girl, the town forgave Little Auntie her beauty. Besides — they would say and still say — couldn't

6

she have been a star herself? And didn't she turn down the chance? To do what women were put here on earth to do . . . And then, very proud, they tell how when she and Uncle Ted were touring the Hollywood studios, Cecil B. De Mille — the great man himself — tried to get them to stay over long enough for Little Auntie to have a screen test, and how she thanked him and said she had other plans (starting a family). And then they tell about the photograph he gave her, to show her children some day — if they doubted her story. (He signed it, "In memory of a beautiful lady." Uncle Ted kept it, alongside one of Little Auntie showing her in profile, wearing a large net hat swathed in yards of sequin-spattered veiling, holding to her face some dark-throated white flowers, translucent with light.)

Little Auntie and Uncle Ted lived only two blocks from my grandparents' house, where Mother and I lived, but for me that two blocks was like a journey into my story books, from a world of heavy oak and dark maroon upholstery and a tight-lipped air of guilt and impending doom to a world of gaudy color and a laughing sense of expectation. Making that journey to that other country, even Mother would speak a different language, a language of idle chatter and large gesture. In that other

7

country, she would lay her hands on my shoulders and tousle my hair and put her arms around me.

Outside, their house was a nondescript wooden bungalow of the 1920s. Inside, it was a homemade, hand-painted version of what she had seen in magazines and movies and of what, out of sheer love of color, she had added — a blend of Moorish, Art Nouveau, and tropical jungle. A proper nest for my dark and lovely aunt.

All of the wood of her furniture she had painted black (the Japanned look); all of the upholstery she had buried in shawls and pillows — pillows of red and purple and pink, pillows of black satin embroidered and appliqued with the same reds and purples and pinks. Across a nondescript table she had draped a silk, fringed Spanish shawl, black with giant red roses.

Her personal leitmotif was birds. And she used them with bravado and humor — embroidered on the pillows, beaded onto a velvet wallhanging, painted onto a fire-screen that concealed, not a fireplace, but an open-flamed gas heater. (It was evident that the lady of the house, despite her exotic plumage, spent her leisure hours as other women of small towns of the flat and dusty plains spent theirs — in needlework and china painting.)

8

On the sideboard in her dining room, where other people had cut-crystal bowls or china tea sets, she had a basket of feathers — from common birds like jays and canaries and from exotic ones like ostriches and egrets. When I would visit her, she would hand them to me, and I would spread them out on the floor, make bouquets of them, tuck them into the collar of my dress where I could rub my chin against them.

In my grandparents' house, the sideboard was no less fascinating — but forbidden. It held Grand-daddy's wonderful-smelling tobacco humidor, his heady-smelling bottles, and the bottles with no smell at all but with pictures of round-faced children in fur hats and fur jackets. These children and their furry garb enthralled me: I would go into the dining room by myself, pull up a chair, climb up on it, and study them and wonder about them. All such study came to an end one day when Nanna found me there, reaching across to one of the bottles. "Just what do you think you're doing?" she hissed, pulling the chair away with such a jerk that I almost fell. "Don't you ever let me catch you up there again!"

There was something very wicked about those children, I concluded. That was the way of things in my grandparents' house: evil hid itself in crystal bottles, on

9

bathroom shelves, and even jumped at you from behind certain words. One had to be very wary. Punishments were frequent; explanations, rare. Not until I was twelve would I learn the secret of the evil hidden in those heady-smelling bottles — Grand-daddy was an alcoholic. How I grieved for the lost innocence of the round-face children; and how happy I was, just this last year, when I encountered them once again, smiling at me from a grocery shelf, from unimpeachable bottles of Cliquot Club soda water. Exonerated, at last.

The summer I was allowed to give up naps, Mother and I, on one of our regular afternoon visits to Little Auntie's house, found her in bed. Surely grown-ups, I thought, don't have to take naps.

The visit did not follow its usual pattern. She did not play what had come to be our little ritual that would begin with her offering me some gum. "Yes, please," I would say. "What kind?" she would ask. "Juicy Fruit, please," I would say. "Juicy Fruit? I don't think I have any." "Well, thank you anyway." Then she would begin to rummage through her bureau drawer, and I would wait, knowing she would soon exclaim in mock surprise,

"What do you know! Juicy Fruit! And some Life Savers, too!" And we would laugh as though none of this had ever happened before.

This time, no offer. No game. No laughter.

The next visit, she was again in bed. And again, no ritual. This time I decided to remind her by initiating it myself. "Have you any gum?" I asked, smiling at my cleverness. Instead of picking up her cue, she turned her head on her pillow, nodded toward the dressing table, and said, "Top-drawer, left-hand side."

Without the game, the prize had lost its savor.

On this, my last visit to her bright nest, there were to be neither smiles nor banter nor hugs.

I was certain it had to do with my asking for the gum.

And even more certain when the next day Mother, leaving for her visit, told me I could not come with her.

For several days she and Nanna made their separate visits, each leaving me behind.

Then, one morning I came across them in one of the downstairs bedrooms — the "company" bedroom — putting fresh sheets on the bed. "Who's coming?" I asked.

"Little Auntie," Mother said.

"To *live* here?" I asked, filling with excitement. It did,

after all, seem thoroughly logical: had not Mother and I come back here to live?

As though she had seen a tarantula on it, Nanna dropped her side of the sheet, drew back, away from the bed.

"I'll finish it, Mama," Mother said quickly. "You go see to the dinner."

Nanna left the room, wringing her hands.

There it is again, I thought, that same wickedness. Where had it come from this time?

Turning round to me, Mother said, "Why don't you see if your grand-daddy needs some help?" She was smiling, trying to make it up to me, I thought, but she was crying at the same time, so I didn't feel much better.

"He's cleaning the Big Car, to go and get Little Auntie," she said.

That made it both better and worse.

The big yellow touring car was the one he used to take me for rides in, those scary, thrilling rides on the brand new road the grown-ups called "the highway" — the air rushing past my face so fast I could hardly catch any of it long enough to breathe — and those funny rides up and down the rises and gullies of dusty country roads, me laughing and squealing and him laughing and looking

12

over at me and yelling, "Tickling your tummy yet?" Those rides that were now forbidden. "Never," Mother had said. "Does that mean 'not ever?'" I asked. "Yes. Not ever," she answered.

As with other crevasses that opened beneath me in that house, there was no explanation; unable to ponder what I had done — or said — I pondered instead that new word, a word I had not had to come to grips with before: *never.*

I did not go the garage, as she suggested. Instead I watched from the dark shade of the back porch as Grand-daddy brushed out the back seat of the big yellow car, as Mother came out with pillows, and as the two of them drove off, Mother at the wheel.

In no time at all, it seemed, I heard Uncle Ted at the front door. Full of expectation, I ran off through the kitchen, across the breakfast room, the dining room . . . when I reached the front entrance, everyone was already there. But no one was smiling. Uncle Ted was carrying Little Auntie.

She did not speak, neither to me nor to anyone.

Thus it continued, day after day. For the first time ever, my beautiful aunt brought none of her light and color to our gray house. Or if she did, I was not allowed to

13

share it; I was kept out of the room. In fact, everywhere I turned, I was unwelcome; Mother, when she was not in the downstairs bedroom with my aunt, looked at me as at some stranger suddenly in her path; Nanna was more brusque than ever; and even Grand-daddy, who seemed never to tire of playing with me and teasing me, would now walk confusedly past me without a word.

I wondered what terrible thing I had done.

It was somewhere in these perplexing days that Ethel first came to our back door. Part of her job, it seemed, along with the cooking and washing and cleaning, was to keep me out from underfoot.

"Come 'long, chile, I be's bilin' the shirts this hyah day," she would say, taking me to the basement, teaching me the secrets of soaking and boiling and bluing and starching. Or, "Fetch the matches for the cinerary." The world seemed to have an unending supply of wonderful words, some quite unsuited to their use: "cinerary," for example, was that piece of chicken wire Grand-daddy had tied into a cylinder to keep the burning trash from blowing down the alley.

Every day after dinner (dinner was at noon) she would

make two huge glasses of lemonade, and, saying to me, "le's be off to our stoop," lead me out the back door, down the shady length of the screened porch, down the steps, past the garage, past the chicken coop, out to the servants' quarters (which we used for garden storage), and there we would sit on the steps in the shade of the catalpa tree, watching the bees in the vitex hedge that separated the quarters from the front lawn, fanning ourselves with palm fans from the First Baptist Church, a gift to the church from the Morton Funeral Home (modestly proclaimed in big letters across each fan).

There, resting, she would reminisce about her childhood as one of eleven children on a sharecropper's farm, about how they had scrubbed the pine floor with lye, put the skillets in red hot ashes to loosen the caked grease, and raked the dusty yard where children's feet had trampled away every blade of grass. All the while we would sit there, happy, drinking our lemonade, fanning ourselves, smelling the vitex on one side, the chicken coop on the other, and occasionally just sitting, listening to the singing at the weekday Bible classes across the alley at the First Baptist Church.

One morning, during this first visitation of Ethel to our house, I awakened to the sound of a house already up and about its business. People talking, moving about, downstairs. And no one had come for me. They don't want me around at all anymore, I thought, they have left me up here, forgotten. Then I saw the clock on the wicker table (with the book, *The Bam Bam Clock,* Grand-daddy had taught me how to tell time). I had not been forgotten; it was still early.

But why was everybody up?

I went downstairs, across the back hall, and into the kitchen.

Nanna was not there. No one was there.

Heading through the breakfast room toward the front of the house, toward the voices, I saw Ethel getting cups and saucers from the cupboard. Everything, it seemed, was out of kilter — Ethel never came until after breakfast.

Cups still in her hands, she placed her solid figure squarely between me and the hall and, taking one of her long rasping breaths, said, "Everybody's done ate, chile." With her hands firmly on my shoulders, she turned me back toward the kitchen. "Ethel calls hersef fixin' you somethin' special."

Bleak and puzzled, I sat down at the kitchen table. I knew she was not telling the truth: the place settings at

16

the breakfast room table were clean and undisturbed, just as they had been laid out the night before by Mother. No one had eaten there.

"Cimmimum toast," Ethel declared proudly, setting before me two pieces of brown, gooey toast still bubbling from the broiler.

As I waited for it to cool, she asked, "Miss Betty ever bury hersef a secret?"

"What?" I had no idea what she was talking about.

"You ain't never buried a secret?"

"No." The word *secret* only deepened my gloom. On my mother's twenty-seventh birthday, Nanna had let me help her wrap the present — a Japanese kimono of yellow and black silk, beautiful enough, I thought, for Little Auntie. As she wrapped it, she told me it was a secret. That being the first time I'd ever heard either the word *secret* or the word *kimono*, I imagined them to be one and the same.

When the time came for the birthday cake, Granddaddy, Mother, Little Auntie, Uncle Ted, and I sat down at the dining room table that I had helped Nanna set, with the dessert plates Little Auntie had bordered with painted flowers and a gold band, with the white damask table cloth (Nanna prided herself that even when she was taking in sewing, she fed her family every day on white linen). The door from the pantry swung open, and in walked Nanna, carrying the birthday cake, all spiky with candles, and I jumped up and cried, "Now we can bring in the kimono!"

Nanna, standing there at the end of the table, holding the cake on its cut-crystal cake stand, tightened her mouth, set the stand firmly down on the table, and — looking as though she had suffered some personal and painful and untreatable injury — walked out of the dining room and across the back hall, where seconds later, we could hear her bedroom door close.

Because of me, because of words I'd said, all of us were sitting there in silent exile, lighting joyless candles.

"A secret?" I repeated, looking up at Ethel with more foreboding than expectation.

"Fust we gots to git ahsefs a secret," she went on. "Soon's you finishes yer toast."

I had other plans. I could hear the voices again, up toward the front of the house, and I started off in their direction. Ethel, moving so quickly she couldn't get enough breath to speak, stepped in front of me and turned me back. "Now," she said, as soon as she had refilled her lungs, "I bet yer grammaw be keepin' a button box."

Nanna had not just one button box but a whole huge drawer of them, each of them brimful with buttons. (I was reared in the belief that only the most slatternly of housewives would fail to keep a button box.)

"Yes," I answered.

"You know where it's at?" she asked.

As these riches had been one of my earliest and favorite toys, I knew exactly where they were. "Upstairs," I said, starting again for the front hall.

"We goes this way," Ethel said, steering me into the back hall.

It was becoming clear to me that no matter what was going on in the front of the house, I was not to be a part of it. Because of something I had done, I supposed.

Up in the sewing room under the eaves, we heard no more voices nor moving around. The only sounds coming to us were the caperings of squirrels jumping from the branches of the mulberry trees onto the roof.

From this room, from these drawers in the tall wardrobe of burl walnut, from this oak veneer sewing machine with the cast-iron treadle and legs, had come all of Little Auntie's exotic clothes.

Crossing to the wardrobe, I pulled out the bottom

drawer, disclosing — with no little pride — Nanna's one-time tools of trade: buttons of cut crystal, of rhinestone, of jet, carved wood, filigreed gilt, and mother-of-pearl. In every size and shape.

"De lawd bless us!" cried Ethel, her eyes devouring the treasure.

Pleased with my power to astonish, I pulled open another drawer, this one filled with trimmings — gold lamé, ecru lace, black lace, embroidered eyelet, rick-rack — and ribbons of velvet and satin and grosgrain and moire. And in one corner, tiny rosebuds made of narrow satin ribbon — saved, I had been told, from the bassinet Nanna had made for her first-born, my mother.

And still another drawer — feathers. For hats.

"Ain't nobody nevah had a secret like we be havin'!" Ethel exclaimed, running her hands across the lustrous velvet, holding the lamé up to the light from the big dormer window.

I was beginning to feel that this time around I might be less of a disappointment in the matter of secrets.

"We needs us a saucer," Ethel said, stretching out the piece of gold lamé.

"I know where," I said getting up to go for one.

"Nevah mind what Miss Betty know," she said, grabbing me by the arm. "She stay right hyah."

And I did, while Ethel went downstairs.

Soon she returned, with a saucer, a salad plate, and a piece of cardboard. "Now we gits down to business," she said.

Spreading out the piece of lamé on the cutting table, she laid the salad plate on it as a pattern and cut out a circle of gold. Then, using the saucer, she cut a circle of cardboard.

"Look keerful," she admonished as she stretched the lamé over the cardboard and, reaching for pins from Nanna's red felt, tomato-shaped pin cushion, pinned the excess margin over the edge and into the back of the cardboard.

"Now we chooses," she said, with a nod toward the drawers, "from all this hyah lot."

I was mystified. Ethel, quiet and intent, selected and discarded, selected and discarded, setting aside small mounds of buttons and trimmings, talking to herself as she fondled her way through the bright horde.

"How come it your ma nevah dig into these hyah?" she asked. She had been a part of our household long enough to have seen on Nanna's walls the pictures of Little Auntie in her fanciful plumage and to have noticed the unobtrusive clothes of my mother.

"Because she has a divorce," I said knowingly, although actually I had no idea where she had it — growing out of a rib or protruding out of an armpit — but I knew it kept her from wearing pretty clothes because I'd heard Nanna say to her, when Mother was trying on one of Little Auntie's dresses, "You can't strut around in clothes like that — not with that divorce!"

Ethel dropped the subject.

Just as I was losing interest in whatever game we were eventually going to play, Ethel closed the drawers and declared, "Now we's ready."

Gathering a handful of crystal buttons, she began placing them one by one on the gold circle — a straight line, breaking off into another, and another, and — "Miss Betty get it yet?" she grinned.

One more line. "A star!" I cried, deciding the game might after all be fun.

Next, in the heart of the star, with iridescent blue buttons, she formed a rosette. Just at that moment, a beam of morning sunlight from the dormer window, having edged its way unnoticed across the cutting table, focussed like a searchlight on our jewelled star, broke apart on the prisms of the crystal buttons, and fell in a rainbow on the golden circle.

Entranced, we watched.

As the beam of light moved ever so slowly on, Ethel brushed her hand roughly across the lamé, flicking the lovely star away.

"Oh-h-h," I cried, distressed, "Why did you do that?"

"Miss Betty's turn," she answered. "How 'bouts this time a flower?" She pointed to some curly white feathers and to some pieces of green ribbon.

I was beginning to understand: it was like the kaleidoscope Uncle Ted brought me from Hollywood, only better, because we made it happen ourselves.

She began to chuckle, "Ethel's secrets ain't nevah held a patch on this un."

"What?" I asked, having no notion what she had said.

"Know what I mos' often uses?"

"Not buttons?"

"Nehi tops, castor beans, leafs, flowers, 'n' foil out'n cigarette packs," she laughed.

We were having a fine time.

Unobserved by us, absorbed as we were now in our acts of creation, the beam of sunlight had moved away from our enchanted gold circle, crossed the room to the wardrobe of burl walnut, and climbed the wall behind it.

When at long last our inventiveness ran out and we had settled on our favorite arrangement, Ethel said, "We be's 'bout ready to bury it now."

"What?" I asked.

"Digs us a hole and puts it in."

"No!" I protested. "It's too pretty. Why can't we keep it?"

"Cuz a secret be's somethin' you don't want nobody to git holt on. It belong to jis us. Miss Betty not to tell, and Ethel not to tell. Then it be's ourn. Jis ourn."

Like the kimono, this secret, too, had begun better than it was ending.

Though dubious, I followed her down the back stairs and to the cleaning closet where, trying several boxes, she settled on one with a pattern of Christmas holly; then, from a drawer where Nanna kept string and rubber bands and the waxy paper from the store bread, Ethel took several pieces of the paper, carefully wrapped our shining secret, laid it in the box, and tied the box with string.

"Now," she announced as though with some finality, "kin you skeer us up a shovel?"

This time I led the way, with Ethel in tow — across the back porch, past the garage, past the chicken coop, out to the servants' quarters, and into its dark interior. Inside the door I stopped, waiting until I could see again. The air was thick with the fumes of fungicides, insect sprays, and box upon box of chicken manure, salvaged by Nanna for her garden. Behind me I heard a choking sound; Ethel's hand pulled loose from mine; I turned, saw her silhouette against the light at the door as she stepped back outside, as she stood there gulping long drinks of fresh air. When she could speak again, she said, "Ethel be took for sure, chile, if she go back in theah. You jis fetch the shovel 'n' come 'long."

Grand-daddy had bought me my own gardening set, and I knew right where to find it. When I came out with the shovel, Ethel was walking along by the vitex hedge, studying the ground. "This hyah is tolable soft," she said, toeing the earth.

I started scraping away, making a shallow trench the way my Grand-daddy and I had done when we planted the zinnia seeds.

"Naw —" Ethel objected. "Leastways ankle-deep."

I sliced into the earth. It was dense and dark; like fudge, I thought, and sliced again, and again, then scooped up a shovelful and tossed it out; more shovels full, and the sides of the hole fell in — looking like cookie mixings in a bowl. Slicing once more, I cut an earthworm in two, stopped to watch its wriggling halves.

I was enjoying myself, quite forgetting our mission, when Ethel's felt house-shoes and cotton stockings came into my line of vision. "Tha's enough," her voice came, and next I saw her hand holding out our well-wrapped secret.

Reluctantly I took it, put it down in the hole, then stepped back, trying to fix in my memory the image of its feathers, its bright star.

"Kiver it," Ethel said.

Half-heartedly, I pushed a little dirt in on top of it.

"Tha's no way," she said, and I saw her feet, in their felt houseshoes, pushing the soil in, stamping it down, then the pink palms of her dark hands, smoothing it out.

I looked up at her.

Straightening up, standing almost tall, she brushed her hands against each other and proclaimed, "This hyah's yers 'n' mine now — ain't nobody else's."

She seemed very proud, and, sad though I was to part with our pretty toy, I felt rather proud, too, as though we had done a fine and worthy thing.

The next morning, I was not left, forgotten, in my

bed. Mother came to awaken me, sat with me while I dressed, sat with me as I ate my breakfast. I had the feeling I was no longer an outcast.

While she washed the dishes, I stood on a low stool Grand-daddy had made for me and dried the silverware. I was very happy, helping Mother, having her all to myself. While she finished wiping the water from the pine counter-top (which was always a little furry with rot), she turned to me and told me that Little Auntie was dead.

I looked up at her, wary, uncomprehending.

Sensing that I did not understand, she said, "It's like being asleep, except for a long while." It was the first time anyone in that house had ever tried to explain to me what their words meant.

I was just hoping it didn't prove to be one of those words that would turn on me, get me into trouble. To stay on the safe side, I made up my mind to be very quiet in my play, to walk softly so as not to awaken her.

Mother was taking off her apron. "I have a surprise for you," she said. "You've been invited to Catherine's house, to spend the day."

Catherine's house . . . where her mother gave us tea parties with a child's tea set! I started off for the hall, running to get my doll to take with me. At the door of the downstairs bedroom, I remembered about Little Auntie being asleep and stopped short, tiptoeing by.

The door was open and I could see into the room. The bed was empty. Wherever she was sleeping, it wasn't here. If she has gone home, I thought, I don't have to worry about waking her up, and with some relief, I skipped off down the hall, clattering along the polished oak flooring.

The next morning, another invitation. The day after that, another. My world was turning sunny and warm — breakfast alone with Mother, going away from our frightening house, and having playmates.

After a few days of this, just as I began to expect that every day after breakfast Mother would announce an invitation, she made a different sort of announcement. "Today we're going to the cemetery," she said.

I began checking through my store of words for a clue: cinerary, cimmimum . . . *cemetery*? I looked a question at her.

"To put flowers on Little Auntie's grave," she explained.

As I went off to brush my teeth, I was hoping Little Auntie would be going with us.

On the back porch Nanna was putting flowers into jars

of water — her canning jars. She handed one jar to me, two to my mother, picked up two herself, and pushing the screen door open with her elbow, led us out to the back driveway. There beside the big yellow touring car, holding the doors open, Grand-daddy was waiting.

We got in, balancing our jars of water and flowers carefully in front of us, and Grand-daddy backed slowly down the driveway. The car smelled like Lela's Flower Shop.

Slow and steady, we drove away, past the First Baptist Church, past the high school and the lumber yard, past all the houses and out beyond the town. But not over those gullies and rises Grand-daddy had once for my amusement turned into a roller coaster; this was a long straight road ending at a flat open place where the earth seemed scoured clean, like a town where all the houses had been blown away, leaving only the streets and a few bushes. And a few blocks of stone.

Where we stopped, there were flowers, lots of flowers, all stacked up and spread out. But wilted. A man was gathering them into a truck.

Out of the box on the running board of the car Grand-daddy lifted something that looked like a doormat and carried it across to the spot where the man was removing the last of the wilted flowers. With our jars, we followed, putting them on the ground beside the mat.

"Give me your pocket knife, Frank," Nanna said.

Taking the knife, getting down on her knees, she began pulling the flowers from the jars, cutting the stems almost to stubs; as she cut them and laid them aside, Mother sorted them by color, into little heaps of red and purple and pink. When they were all cut, Nanna, closing the knife and getting shakily to her feet, said, "I just can't do it, Alice. You'll have to do it."

Mother, kneeling down before the mat, picked out a handful of pink zinnias and began sticking them into it, in a long sweep of a line — like a bird's wing, I thought; then she sat back on her heels, studied it, frowned, took them out, started a straight line.

I stood watching, intent. "Try a star," I suggested.

She looked up at me. I have surprised her, I thought.

"Would you like to help?" she asked.

"Yes," I said. Proud and excited, thinking how I would now really surprise her, I began a starburst of purple ageratum.

"Why, Betty! You're going to be an artist!" she exclaimed.

"That's what I keep telling you, Alice," Nanna put in.

30

Aware that I was the center of attention, I added line after line, recreating in flowers all the trial patterns Ethel and I had made in buttons and feathers and sequins, using only the patterns we had discarded, being careful not to repeat the one we had settled on — our final, secret pattern.

I heard a snuffling noise, coming from Nanna. "If only your Little Auntie could see it!" Then, the same snuffling sound from Mother.

I was laying out a line of pinks . . . I stopped. There it is, I thought. Even out here, away from the big, gray rooms. The same old wickedness that never wears a face of its own but always hides itself in the nicest faces anyone could imagine — like those happy children on Grand-daddy's bottles. And now, even these pretty flowers.

"Why can't we take it home for her to see?" I suggested, hoping to make up for whatever had gone wrong.

But it wasn't working; I could tell by the looks they were exchanging — all three of them now. Grand-daddy, standing off to one side, was saying, "I told you. I told you the child didn't understand."

Mother, looking stern and sharp at Nanna. "And you saying she was a hard-hearted little thing. 'Hadn't shed a tear,' you said."

While I sat there among the flowers, afraid even to touch them, just listening, the three of them shuffled the blame, the blame for something I had done — something that wasn't my fault but someone else's. They couldn't agree as to whose.

Then they started talking about how I didn't understand, but this, too, seemed the fault of somebody else. And of words. Words someone should have explained to me.

On and on they argued, while I looked at the zinnias, then at the pinks, and finally at their feet — feet that were doing lots of moving about but still managing to stand in one spot — Mother's black patent pumps, Nanna's laced shoes with the pointed toes, Granddaddy's funny-looking, fat-toed, high-ankled shoes.

Now Mother was crying again, and her pumps stepped off to the side; Grand-daddy was swearing at Nanna, and her shoes went away entirely.

By now they had said enough that I was no longer looking either at the flowers or at their feet. Instead, my eyes were fixed on the ground out in front of those feet, where the wilted flowers had lain: freshly raked, without grass or weeds, like the ground under the vitex hedge after Ethel had stamped it down in her felt houseshoes. And there — I was trying to imagine it, trying to fit it into the patterns of those things I knew, to find a place among them for this new thing, this terrible thing — that there, in that ground in front of me, lay my dark and lovely aunt.

Buried. Just like the bright secret Ethel and I had buried under the hedge.

Buried, moreover, by those feet that were just now beginning to encircle me.

I felt Grand-daddy's strong hands under one shoulder, Mother's under the other, and though I do not really know, cannot remember, I think I began to scream. Most certainly, I struggled against those lifting hands.

I was afraid of their hands, afraid of their feet — I was afraid of *them*.

I do not know when Ethel left.

Though she came to our house three other times — at Grand-daddy's death, at Mother's, at a great uncle's — I was in school then, and she would come to work after I had left in the morning and would be gone when I came back in the afternoon.

During the lunch hour I would see her, fleetingly. Except when Mother lay dying — then I hardly saw her at all because, as soon as Nanna and I would sit down to lunch, Ethel would go to Mother's room and stay there until we finished. As with the visitors who came to see Mother in her last weeks, Nanna was terribly jealous. "What do you talk about in there, Ethel?" she would ask. Her excuse for this possessiveness, as with the visitors, was "It just takes her strength." As though Mother's strength were something she needed to hoard — for the final business of dying.

Whatever Mother told Ethel, or Ethel told Mother, Ethel never revealed. It was a secret, and remained, just between them.

Now Nanna lies in the hospital, paralyzed by a stroke, and Ethel has once again appeared at our back door, for this, the last of the last illnesses.

Having to be in school or at the hospital, I see little of her, but she cooks for me and gets the house in order for what she takes for granted is coming — the funeral.

After the other funerals, the living — as soon as they could — got around to the business of shaping the house to the lives left in it. This time is different. This time, the funeral is not just for Nanna; it is for the house and the lives it has stood for.

Now, the house has finished with us.

After the other funerals, it had been up to Nanna to let Ethel know when she was no longer needed. This time it will be up to me.

But first, there is the business of the house; it, too, deserves a decent burial.

Night after night I walk its rooms, memorizing all that I must leave behind, choosing the little I can take with me. What is to become of mother's furniture that, after all the years of waiting in the attic, was never called again to a home of its own? Of Nanna's sewing machine that in the early years kept the family in food and, during the later years, Little Auntie in her finery?

Among the things I put aside to take with me are Little Auntie's long sequin-spattered veiling, Mother's Japanese kimono, Grand-daddy's humidor, and the needlework — the doilies, pillow cases, tablecloths, and even handkerchiefs — on which Nanna and Little Auntie and Mother had lavished their lives.

Each night, when the stories of the rooms become sadder than I can bear, I go up to the sewing room and there, sitting on the floor, I sort Nanna's buttons. After sorting a few piles, I string them and lay them on the cutting table. For many nights I do this, because I am coming around to the realization that though I can walk away from these rooms full of thoroughly useful furnishings, I cannot walk away from these strings of useless baubles.

On Ethel's last day, after I have given her a last check and a last bonus, after we have said our good-byes, I follow her out, down the length of the back porch to the screen door. As always, she is spending more effort in breathing than in talking. When she reaches the door, she turns back and grins, her head hung low, looking up at me askance as she always has, and starts out the door and down the steps.

"Ethel!" I call, as though already she were at a great distance.

She turns back.

"Ethel . . . do you remember our secret? Out under the vitex?"

"Yes'm, Miss Betty."

"Do you really, Ethel?" I am holding on hard — why should she? I wonder — she who was just doing her duty as a nursemaid; I was the one who was the impressionable child . . . "Do you suppose it's still there?" I ask, still holding on.

"Who be diggin' it up?" she asks. "I never tole. Did you be tellin'?"

"No." I can think of no more to say. Then, "No. I've never told. It's still our secret."

"Yes'm, Miss Betty; it's jis ourn." She looks at me more directly than she has ever done. "They's nobody lef' what knows the things we knows."

THE SUMMER NO ONE WAS POOR

THAT WHOLE SUMMER LONG, it all made sense. Everything. The whole world. From Ninth Street to Eleventh, from Ash Street to Cedar. Living, as I did, at the world's axis (Tenth and Birch), I was in a position to know. Besides, I checked it out, house by house, every evening. (Heaven, however, I left to get by on its own, feeling it was in good hands — what with Jesus and Prometheus both up there, waiting around, asking God all the time, When do we get to come back? And with Little Auntie waiting, too, peering down at Uncle Ted and Nanna and Grand-daddy and Mother and me, waiting for the day when we would join her up there where the summers weren't so hot.)

Meanwhile, down here, we did have Grover Higgins to contend with. But he, too, could be accounted for in the general scheme of things, right alongside the Devil

— their job being to keep the rest of us on our toes.

As for my job, I helped my lean, white-haired, blue-eyed grandfather, who looked like he'd wandered onto the frontier by mistake — with what Nanna called his "terrible waste" and what Mother called his "demonic refusal" to accept the fact that when God said the earth should bring forth abundantly, He had not seen western Oklahoma.

Not that God was any help to Grand-daddy. In fact, Grand-daddy delighted in pointing to the brown, dried-up bermuda grass of his neighbors' yards and saying to the preacher, "That's how it is when God's going it alone." No, Grand-daddy's success in the garden could be attributed solely to his extravagance and his per-severance — for every five things that we reaped, we had sowed twenty-five. In this country so dry the creekbeds were more often filled with blowing sand than with flowing water, Grand-daddy and I planted and watered and weeded, watched some of it grow, lots of it die — yet still had wagons full to give away.

All of which led to my second job, as operator of a neighborhood exchange-and-delivery service — a ser-vice conceived by Grand-daddy and dedicated to the proposition that enough is never as good as too much.

Serving all the houses on both sides of the street, one block in each direction from Tenth and Birch, the exchange (callcd the Daily Deliverance) was run by me and Lee Ann Anderson and was kept perpetually provided by the exuberance and the excesses of my grandfather — without whose prodigalities our service, no doubt, would have been limited to the housewifely exchange of a cup of borrowed sugar or the proud gift of a jar of jelly.

The rolling stock of our neighborhood exchange consisted of the Tenth Street Terror and the Daily Deliverance, from which the service derived its name. The Tenth Street Terror was a scooter that Grand-daddy himself had built for me, a scooter "once seen, never forgotten," he said. The wheels were ball-bearing roller skates; the front of it (the part, that is, connecting the two-by-four handlebar to the footboard) was an orange crate painted strawberry pink on the outside and sweet-pea lavender on the inside. "Sissy Cart" is what Grover Higgins called it, but that was because he was jealous, Mother assured me — *his* scooter being just a plain, store-bought metal one, with ordinary, rubber-tire wheels.

Though the shelf inside the orange crate was adequate

for small deliveries, it was not up to the man's work of hauling Grand-daddy's excesses — seedlings, potted plants, cut flowers, cucumbers, corn, magazines, and books (subscribing to everything from seed catalogues to book clubs, he was also a one-man lending library); so he built a wagon, the Daily Deliverance, to hook onto the back of the Terror. With its wooden slats and iron-banded wheels, the Deliverance resembled the wagons the farmers used for transporting their females, their children, and their cotton to town on Saturdays; but, while their wagons were weathered and rusted, the Daily Deliverance was painted the green of the Mistletoe Express wagon down at the depot and was garlanded with honeysuckle vines. "Fit for a wedding coach," Grand-daddy would proclaim, as he twined the last tendrils of honeysuckle through the slats and sent us on our evening rounds. When Grover Higgins got his first look at it, he fell down, laughing, right in the Adamses' front yard — "Because he's so jealous," Mother explained.

The Daily Deliverance never rolled until Grand-daddy and I finished our early-evening gardening, which always began after he drained and then refilled his enormous half-quart goblet of iced tea (which, strangely, he never let me taste, like Nanna and Mother let me taste theirs). Taking the refilled goblet with him, leaving Nanna and Mother to their kitchen chores, he would lead the way, through the back porch and out to the garden. There, working side by side, we would talk. With most people, talking was something I'd given up the year before, when I was four, but with Grand-daddy the words found their way with no trouble at all, just tumbling out as easy as anything.

While I let the cool mud ooze up between my bare toes and watched the thick brown water suds up like the melted marshmallows in my hot chocolate, he would point out the flowers that wanted their heads in the sun, the ones that wanted their feet dry, the ones that had been brought from across the ocean years and years ago — and then he would explain to me what an ocean was.

One evening he showed me how he had brushed the yellow powder from the center of one flower to the center of another, and how from this he had grown the sweet-faced Betty Janes, which he had then named after me. This was a story I accepted as true and sensible, just as I accepted all that I heard and saw that summer when everything — even Grover Higgins — made sense.

While in the evenings Grand-daddy was teaching me about plants and oceans and the virtues of chicken manure, in the daytime Mother, hoping I'd find my tongue again, was administering elocution lessons to me — in large doses. These lessons consisted of having me memorize — by repeating after her, one line at a time — a whole repertoire of stories, ranging from B'rer Rabbit to Greek myths. Between Grand-daddy's lessons and the myths, my mind got stretched so wide that my Sunday School teacher took pains to warn me about the Devil — it seems I made no proper distinction between God and Zeus, referred to them, in fact, interchangeably. How could I tell her — even had I been more of a talker — that both of them, it seemed to me, were spiteful and unpredictable old men that a person would do well to steer clear of? As between Prometheus and Jesus, I did better. And worse. Which is to say, I could tell them apart, but I took more of a liking to Prometheus who, just for us, carried that fire all the way from Heaven in his bare hands . . . and the only thanks he got from Zeus was to get nailed onto that mountain and sending that big bird to keep pecking at him forever and forever.

"Inhuman, that's what it is," Nanna would declare as Mother and I subjected ourselves to our daily round of memorizing, her taking me through a story, over and over and over, until I learned it. The fact of the matter was that nothing — not even the pivotal neighborhood role conferred on me by the Daily Deliverance service — made me as proud as feeling a new story growing in me, line by line, building toward the evening when I would stand, barefooted, on the raised dais of the dahlia bed and announce to Grand-daddy, "I know a new story," when I would watch his face as he looked at me, declaring, in mock dismay, *"Another* one? *Already?"*

While I stood there, smiling, waiting — like the travelling vaudeville players that came to the Palace — he would find a level spot for his iced-tea glass, rush off for a lawn chair, lug it to the north side of the dahlia bed, and then, excusing himself as he stepped across in front of all the imaginary theatregoers, he would take his seat and wait politely for the performance to begin.

As soon as it ended, he'd be on his feet, clapping, declaring me his Scheherazade of the Shastas. At such moments, it seemed no more than fitting that a flower should be named after me.

We always loaded the Deliverance under the big mulberry tree behind the back porch, where the rays of the setting sun had to crawl along the ground to find us, making shadows so long and skinny they stretched all the way over to the house and up the high foundation.

One evening Grand-daddy, looking up into the tree, said, "Let's see how high you can climb." While he went back and forth, loading the wagon, I made my way up into the big mulberry — through its large low branches where the sunlight was only an occasional splotch, through a tangle of branches growing ever smaller, into gray light growing ever dimmer — on I climbed, high, coming at last into a leafy pocket of quiet and dark. There I stopped. And listened to the world. Out on Tenth Street, a car went by. Somewhere, a door opened and closed. Soon Grand-daddy called, "Ready to roll!"

From my leaf-shrouded shelter, I could see only his shoes and the bottoms of his trousers.

"Hey there!" he called. I didn't move. Or answer.

"You there! You playing hide-and-seek?"

I held my breath . . . feeling I had a new, magic power: the power to make myself invisible.

When I leaned my head out into the light, I could see him squinting up through the layers of shade, like he was looking into the full sun. "Well, I'll be a jack-rabbit!" he exclaimed, catching sight of me.

As I climbed down, he told me, "Even the Devil

couldn't find you — not up there. So don't you forget it, in case he ever comes for you."

Or Grover Higgins, more like, I thought. And decided it might, indeed, be worth remembering.

Lee Ann Anderson, watching from across the street where *every night* she and her sister and mother had a picnic supper out in the side yard of the Adamses' house where they lived — like Mother and I lived with Nanna and Grand-daddy, was the way I supposed — would run over and join us when she saw us starting to load.

When at last, just as the light was growing gray and peachy and lavender, Lee Ann and I would maneuver our clumsy caravan out onto the sidewalk and head out for our rounds, keeping an alert eye out for Grover Higgins; Grand-daddy, climbing into his big yellow touring car, honking and waving, would head down the driveway and off on *his* evening rounds, his, too, being, I supposed — though I had no idea what they consisted of — just another part of the well-run Providential scheme.

In my memory, at least, those nightly caravans have accumulated all the accoutrements, all the glory of a triumphant procession — with the strawberry-pink-and-lavender Tenth Street Terror and with the Mistletoe-Express-green Daily Deliverance garlanded with hon-

49

eysuckle vines and loaded with flowers and vegetables and books, with Lee Ann and me walking as proud as two conquering Caesars returning to Rome with the spoils of war, greeted by the expectant populace — out watering their yards, rocking on their front porches, gossiping with their neighbors — all waving their welcomes to us, and the lightning bugs just coming out, flashing us on our way.

Every life lived along that route we knew or supposed we knew — how the Bensons were the last people to finish their suppers, how Mrs. Harris called out every evening to Mr. Harris as he watered his small front yard, "Don't forget the parking, John."

Almost every evening someone would give us food "for poor old crippled Miz Karney," a widow confined to a wheel chair. On the Fourth of July we arrived at her house with a slice of devil's food cake from Mrs. Harris, a piece of blackberry cobbler from Mrs. Sims, ham and black-eyed peas from Nanna, two kinds of cole slaw, and four kinds of potato salad. As soon as she'd see us coming, she'd get all teary, and as often as not she'd send us back with tatted lace or crocheted antimacassars or embroidered dish towels "for all those dear people."

Another regular was Old Ned, who lived in the room

attached to the Simses' garage. Because Old Ned was a great storyteller, we kept his stop for last. He'd be sitting out on his front stoop (a slab of broken concrete) on a straight-backed, rope-bottomed chair, with a big white onion in one hand and a pocket knife in the other, and when he saw us coming down the Simses' driveway, he'd start slicing off a couple of fresh wedges of that onion, like off an apple, and when we got up to the stoop, he'd hold out a wedge for Lee Ann and a wedge for me — all wet and shiny, with the juice running out over the knife and onto his fingers.

In his line of work (he mowed yards), I guess he didn't get to do much talking, and he must have missed it, because he sure did a lot of it when we stopped in. Some tales he could go on and on about, like the days when he was a boy, and about his mother and his father and his five brothers and three sisters and the farm they left in Kentucky and how good it all was and how there'd never been anything like it since. Some few stories in particular he kept coming back to, as if he thought that if he kept working at them until he got them ringing real true, then maybe he could bring it all back. After each telling, Lee Ann and I would end up as happy and as full of grins as the first time, and he'd end up as full of sighs. It had to do with being a grown-up, I supposed.

That's the way it was, all that summer long.

Then, when school started and Lee Ann went off to Jefferson Grade School, Mother decided that getting rid of my tonsils was more important than learning to read. "She can catch up," she said, justifying her decision to Nanna. But the hundred-degree weather, the doctor said, was not a good time for operations, so as it turned out, we had to wait so long that I didn't start school at all that year.

In late October, with the weatherman reporting a Norther on the way, Grand-daddy drove Mother and Nanna and me to Oklahoma City in Nanna's big, high-off-the-road, royal-carriage-like Cadillac, with the gray plush on the seats and up the walls and across the ceiling and a bud vase on each side of the back windows — the car Grand-daddy had bought Nanna, with his first oil money, at the same time that he bought himself the big yellow touring car.

After the operation Grand-daddy returned to Dixter, while Nanna and Mother and I stayed over, quite a few days, them taking turns — one staying with me, feeding me ice cream and playing games, and the other one going shopping in the big-city department stores.

When the time came to return home, it was not Grand-daddy who came for us in the big Cadillac. It was Uncle Ted. I was disappointed.

Driving home, wrapped in a blanket in the back seat because winter had come, looking at the carnation Nanna had put in one of the bud vases just for me, I saw a brownish-red stain, the size of a cup, on the gray plush ceiling of the car. It hadn't been there on the trip up.

"What's that?" I complained, indignant that anyone could have been so careless of our grand and beautiful car.

"Just a stain," said Nanna.

But how did it get up *there?* I wondered; anything *I* ever spilled always fell to the floor — never to the ceiling . . . .

"Look over there!" Uncle Ted burst out, pointing at a nursing calf. And suddenly everyone acted like maybe I'd never seen a nursing calf before. I kept looking back up at that ugly brown-red stain.

And I've always thought that, if I could only have figured out or been told what it was and how it came to be there, that maybe I wouldn't have stopped talking all over again — like they said I did, and which bothered Mother a lot but didn't bother me at all, anymore than being invisible up in the mulberry tree.

But they didn't tell me. Nobody told me. Not then, and almost not ever.

Still, if they had, if they had just said, That's your Grand-daddy's blood up there, in the gray plush, and it won't wash away; your Grand-daddy had an accident and the car rolled over and his head was hurt and he's not the same and he's not ever going to be the same; he'll just drink more iced tea (which isn't iced tea, they might have said).

But of course they didn't know all that yet, not even them — Mother and Nanna and Uncle Ted — they didn't know yet how he would change; although the doctor would tell Nanna, "Likely it'll be the one he loves the most . . . ." she just thought that meant it would be her. They had yet to learn all that. And even as they were trying to learn, they went on, for the longest time, blaming it all on the iced tea.

But they said nothing to me, not even about the tea, and so I wouldn't learn until after Grand-daddy and Mother and Uncle Ted were all in their graves and Nanna soon to be in hers, and she said something about "that time your Grand-daddy turned over in the Cadil-lac . . ." and told me all about it. By then it was too late.

But at the time I didn't think too long about the meaning of the stain. In my eyes it was to be what happened to the tree that was the sign — the sign that the world had gone suddenly dangerous.

When we got home, it was dark, and Grand-daddy had already left on his rounds. I was disappointed.

I saw the tree before breakfast the next day. Going to the back screened porch to get the milk and eggs (in cool weather Nanna didn't waste ice on food that could as well be put out on the porch), I opened the kitchen door and saw it. Or what was left of it.

"Close the door!" Nanna called. "You're letting in the cold air!" Because I was just standing there, in the open door, staring at what had been my big wonderful hiding tree.

Stepping outside, out onto the porch, I closed the door. And went on staring — straight through the tree's bare branches.

All its leaves were gone. Vanished. My tree was ruined. Forever.

And Grover Higgins, of course, had done it. Not even noticing the cold, I stood there, grieving, for my tree, trying to imagine the wickedness that could do such a thing. *Every leaf.*

Pulling Grand-daddy's tool-box over to the edge of the porch, I stepped up onto it, so I could see over the solid part of the wall that held up the screening — then I saw the leaves, all in a heap on the ground. With all the green gone out of them. As ugly and brown as the dark stain in Nanna's Cadillac.

It must have taken Grover Higgins all day, I thought.

Nanna was yelling at me, from inside the kitchen, saying I mustn't stay out in the cold, with no wrap and my tonsils not long out.

I went back into the kitchen. Looked at Nanna, looked at Mother, hoping they could say something to make it all right, all the while knowing they couldn't — they couldn't get all those leaves back, not even if they were still green and beautiful. And worse — knowing nothing could ever be right, with Grover Higgins running loose, right in our own back yard.

Neither of them said a word, just went on about the business of breakfast, as though they hadn't noticed — even Nanna, who never missed a thing, even when you wished she would.

I went into the breakfast room. Though usually Grand-daddy had eaten before I was up, his place was still untouched, just the way it had been laid out the night before.

"Where's Grand-daddy?" I called to Nanna, in the kitchen. "Asleep," she replied, in a loud whisper, "and keep your voice down."

Grand-daddy asleep? But, of course, I realized, he has to sleep, just like other people. But I'd never seen him at it.

Then I heard Mother, not bothering to whisper, "Let her raise holy hell, for all I care — serves him right."

"Alice!" Nanna didn't approve of swearing — even if Grand-daddy did do a lot of it.

After breakfast Mother put me to work at a new jigsaw puzzle she had bought for me in Oklahoma City. Along toward lunchtime I heard Grand-daddy and Nanna in the kitchen — he was angry. But before I had a chance to listen, Mother was at my side, taking me by the hand, pulling me into the front entrance hall, wrapping me in a coat and scarf. "Want to visit Old Ned?" she asked.

"Yes!" Old Ned . . . *he* would cheer me up, telling me one of his tales. Besides, since Lee Ann had been in school and since the dark had been coming so early, the Daily Deliverance hadn't even been out of the garage — not once. Though Mother had explained to me that when school was over, next spring, the early dark would go away, she didn't realize that, with so few years behind me, the sequence of seasons was something I didn't properly understand.

As we waited in the cold, on Old Ned's stoop, listening to his screen door rattling in the wind, Mother saying, "Seems like this racket would drive him crazy," we heard his voice, coming, it seemed, from a long way off — though it couldn't have been with him having (if Mother was right) just the one room.

"Who is it?" the voice came.

"Alice and Betty Jane," answered Mother.

"Jis give it a push. It hain't got a lock," he replied, still a long way off.

Inside, it was dark. Right in the middle of the day. The roller shades were pulled down; and besides, there were only two windows, small ones.

My eyes wandered around the darkness looking for Ned.

"Turn on the light," his voice came, "there by the door, there's a switch."

58

When it came on, a bare bulb hanging from a cord and me looking straight into it, I was blinded, like looking up into the sun; so I still couldn't find Ned.

When I found him, right there in front of me — or rather found his face, peering at us from a heap of bed clothes, his head wrapped in what looked like a sweater, with the arms about where his ears should have been — it didn't look like Ned's face. It had white blotches. Then I saw that the blotches were really a patchy growth of whiskers.

"I brought two hot-water bottles," Mother said, "and some hot soup and corn bread." She started running water into a blackened enamel pan she picked up from the single gas burner (sitting on a card table) connected with a rubber hose to the gas hookup at the floor.

"Why don't you light your stove?" I asked, shivering, looking over at an old gas heater with broken radiants.

"'Fraid I'll 'phyxiate," he answered.

"What?"

"Like you and I turn off our heaters and open our windows when we go to bed," Mother explained.

"Why are you in bed?" I asked, because, after all, it wasn't night.

"To keep warm," he answered.

"But if you got up, you could keep the heater turned on." Mother's face was sending me signals . . . I hushed.

On the way home she explained that Old Ned was in bed because the cold weather brought on his rheumatism.

"Then why doesn't he light the fire?" I persisted.

"Because in the winter he has no work and can't afford the fire. So he stays in bed — to keep warm — and because his rheumatism hurts."

Even I could see that it was a wicked arrangement . . . and, as near as I could figure, it wasn't Grover Higgins's fault. And I couldn't see how the Devil had anything to do with it, either.

When we walked in the back door at home, Nanna said, "You forgot to take Mrs. Karney's."

"No, I didn't," Mother retorted. "It's enough to make me gag — just to step inside her front door."

"Very well," Nanna said, her voice sharp. "I'll take it myself."

"Why do you gag?" I asked.

"Didn't you and Lee Ann ever go inside?" Mother asked.

"No." By the time we would get to her house — way down the block — she had already wheeled herself onto her front porch.

"Well, it stinks. God-awful. Like an outdoor privy."

"Stinks?"

"Now, Alice," Nanna was buttoning her coat, "she shouldn't be blamed for what she can't help."

"What can't she help?" I asked.

"Wetting all over everything she sits on," Mother said.

Nanna said nothing, just picked up the soup and corn bread and went out the back door — closing it louder than she had to.

Then Mother explained Mrs. Karney's problem. Another wicked arrangement.

Back at my jigsaw puzzle in the living room, I heard a car drive in over the crunchy gravel of the back driveway — Grand-daddy, at last. Jumping up, I ran through the dining room, across the breakfast room and was coming around the corner into the kitchen, running so fast I slid on the slippery linoleum — and there he was, coming through the door at the opposite end of the kitchen.

"Grand-daddy!" I called, still running, throwing my arms out wide. He kept coming, straight toward me, like he was going to run me down; I hopped to the side, laughed and turned, caught up with him again, slowed to a walk, went along beside him into the breakfast room, looking up, grinning, waiting for him to quit teasing me, to turn and grab me up and say, "Why look who's here — why didn't you speak up?"

So, laughing, I stepped out in front of him, waving at him. "Mr. Kelso, *sir!*" I said.

He didn't look down. He didn't stop.

"Want to see where my tonsils used to be?"

"Not now," he said, not looking down at me, just looking out in front of him, answering me as though I might have called from another room.

I can't have made him angry, I thought, I haven't even seen him. In fact, I couldn't remember his ever having been angry with me. Disgusted, yes, the time I was afraid to go down the big slide in the park down in Dallas. After that I never let on if I was scared, not even the day he asked to see how high I could climb in the mulberry.

Day after day I resorted to everything that once had pleased him — even to announcing that I knew a new story. It wasn't that he was unkind; it was rather that he was unseeing. I had become as invisible as I had been the day I hid among the thick dark leaves of the mulberry tree. But now it gave me no sense of magic or of power.

The world went on like that. Nothing making good sense anymore. I wasn't even too upset when I learned the reason for Lee Ann and her sister and her mother having a picnic every night last summer out in the Adamses' side yard — me thinking she was the luckiest girl in the world, and all the time it was because they didn't live in the Adamses' house the same way Mother and I lived in Nanna's and Grand-daddy's but, instead, just rented two sleeping rooms and a bathroom and didn't have a living room or a dining room or even a kitchen.

Then one night something happened. I don't know what it was; it seemed already to have happened when I heard them. I was asleep, upstairs. What time it was I don't know, but Nanna had been to bed because she was in her nightgown and bathrobe; they were talking so loud they woke me, and after I got awake enough to listen I couldn't understand what they were saying because they were all talking at once, only Grand-daddy and Mother weren't really talking, they were yelling.

I seemed to know at once that whatever was happening might be happening to me.

Slipping out into the darkness of the upstairs hall, I looked over the bannister. And saw them, down in the light of the downstairs hall lamp, with the dark all around them — Nanna, in her night clothes, saying,

"Now, Frank . . ." putting both hands up against his shoulders like she was trying to turn him around, Grand-daddy in his trousers and big heavy sweater like he had just come in, and Mother all dressed up because earlier that night she had gone to a party.

But who was the other person? The man. What was he doing there? A man I'd never seen before, who wasn't saying anything, was just standing there looking like he wished he could be somewhere else. The light from the hall lamp reflected off something on his shirt, like it reflected off Nanna's glasses, except this looked like a Christmas tree ornament — shiny and silver. A star . . .

Mother was saying, "I won't stand for it," and Grand-daddy was saying, "And what do you think you'll do about it?" and Mother was saying, "I'll take Betty Jane and go away — that's what I'll do . . . ." and then Nanna saying, "Now, Alice . . ." and the man looking at one and then the other. And then Mother said the terrible thing, after Grand-daddy had asked her what she'd do, and she'd said take me away; and then he said, "What will you take her *in?*" And that's when she said it, said, "I'll put her in the Deliverance and pull her down the street in the middle of the night if I have to — but I won't stay here — and I won't let her stay here either."

64

At once I knew what I must do. I knew I must run and hide. Because I could see how it was to be — Mother and me out in the cold and the dark, her pulling me down the street, with no place to go.

But how was I to get out? The backstairs — because its scurryings and squeakings gave me nightmares — was always locked from both ends at my bedtime. So the only way out of the house from upstairs was to go through that lighted hall where Grand-daddy and Mother were yelling about what she could and couldn't do.

Then I remembered — it wouldn't be of any use, getting out of the house. Because my hiding tree was gone.

So, in the end, I hid in the closet of the sleeping porch, shivering there, all night.

In the morning, right after breakfast, I went to the garage. Pulling the Daily Deliverance out, I rolled it around behind the garage, past the chicken coop, and pushed it in between the chicken coop and the fence that was covered with ugly brown vines and weeds.

Then, going back to the garage, I got two of the empty gunnysacks Grand-daddy kept to make shade for the plants that didn't like their heads in the sun. Taking them to the mulberry tree, I filled them with the brown and ugly leaves from under my tree, dragged the filled sacks back to the chicken coop, emptied them, placed the gunny sacks over the Daily Deliverance, then, armful by armful, scattered the leaves over the gunny sacks. When I finished, nothing was visible but a mound of brown leaves.

It didn't stop Mother from taking me away. Or from staying away — long enough that I learned about seasons.

When we came back at last, Grand-daddy was dead. And the Daily Deliverance was gone. I never learned what happened to it.

WHEN MOTHER PLAYED MOONSHINE

PULSING THROUGH THE OPEN DOOR of the First Baptist Church, Mendelssohn's *Wedding Recessional* was bestowing an extraordinary pomp on the ordinary business of walking to work. All up and down the block, the townspeople, passing into the reverberating shade of the Chinese elms and the catalpas, lifted their feet to the beat of the march, carried themselves with a sense of ceremony.

Inside the church, Mrs. Davis was pumping away at the organ in rehearsal for a wedding, her ample bottom overflowing the bench, unaware that she was conferring this note of celebration on the summer morning.

A note that was only fitting. We were, after all, witnessing a miracle. Like the one in "Sleeping Beauty" was the way it seemed to me. Though I had long since forsaken fairy tales (I was now thirteen years old), they had not forsaken me. Trailing their clouds of immortality, they had simply been reincarnated in romances and religion: from Sleeping Beauty returning to life, it wasn't too broad a leap to King Arthur returning from Avalon or to the entire congregation of the First Baptist Church rising from beneath their gravestones on the Great Gettin' Up Mornin' . . . .

And now, Mother, who a few weeks ago was not to have lived through the night — here she was, smiling, enthroned in the wide-winged cane rocking chair out on our big front porch, sitting there at the top of the broad stairs like a princess on a dais, framed on either side by grand and lacy curtains of Virginia creeper vines.

And there, out on the sidewalk, their steps quickening to the music, were the courtiers, roused once more to life. At first, oblivious to the miracle. Then, as one by one they noticed Mother sitting there on the high porch, camouflaged in a leafy pattern of light and shade where sunlight shimmered its way through the vines onto her face and arms and dress, and onto the white frame wall of the house behind, the cadence of their steps would falter, until — certain of what they were seeing — they would turn into our walk and climb the long, broad steps of the porch, bearing gifts of gladness on their faces.

To those less steeped in fantasy, the props may have appeared mundane: the cane throne, the cement dais, the seersucker and linen and gingham of the courtiers' robes. No matter. The princess herself was not at her best. Her left arm rested, limp, on a pillow. And she was shy one breast.

The celebration was not without its cynics. A mother jay, whose young were hidden in a nest somewhere in the vines, kept sounding a loud tocsin, fussing and squawking, fretting and fluttering, while Nanna, ignoring the organ and marching to the jay's alarm, kept appearing and disappearing and reappearing from inside the house, banging the screen door as she came and went, plumping the pillow under Mother's arm, pushing her chair into the breeze . . . to her this day had nothing to do with courtiers or well-wishers; to her it was Peach Canning Day — one of those self-flagellating orgies with which Nanna held at bay the omnipresent wickedness of the world. So, despite all her solicitous clucking, she saw to it that Mother was provided with a knife, two pans, and — at her side — a bushel basket heaped high with rosy, fuzzy peaches.

The first to make his way up our walk and up the broad steps was thin, white-haired, white-suited Dr. Williams, who, for all the years I could remember, had passed our house four times a day, never omitting a formal tip of his hat to anyone in sight (panama in summer, gray felt in winter), yet never venturing a single word of greeting. Now even he, importuned by the occasion, came up, hat in one hand, the other held out to Mother. "Good to see you."

Having said as much, he seemed at a loss, and so he repeated, "Yes, good to see you." Mother, for her part, seemed to take this as a full, adequate, and heart-felt statement.

Next came huge, rolling Mrs. Sims from across the street. Hanging out the wash, she had seen Dr. Williams turn in and, peering between the shirts and underwear, had spied Mother. So, abandoning her wash in its wicker basket, she heaved her way across the street, a toothpick in her mouth, her hair in kid curlers, her feet in felt house shoes, her three hundred pounds in a sacklike cotton dress. Out of breath, she paused for wind before climbing the steps and then, lifting her heft slowly up each step, said to Mother, "Well, I see your ma's already put you to work. That's the way."

This was her only allusion to the wonder of Mother's return, for Mrs. Sims's conversation was rarely tailored to suit the occasion: it had its own format and its own content, unsullied by mere births, funerals, or miracles. "You s'pose ole Miz Davis'll ever git that piece learnt?" Too wide for the rockers, she sat on the wooden swing — while I sneaked an anxious look at the ceiling it was suspended from. "I've heerd snappier from the Salvation Army." From this she went on to the subject of her husband's gassy stomach, to the gall between her legs where her fat thighs rubbed themselves raw ("I just have to keep dabbing them with soda"), and to her daughter's latest pregnancy — the unmarried daughter who, with two children by a previous unmarriage, lived at home with her parents. "I tole Jim, I says, 'It seems like we have more than our share of miracles. Where do they come from?' I says. The girl h'aint a friend in this world, man or woman!"

She probably fell asleep on a bus, I thought. Even *I* knew better than that, than to sleep with men, that is. (In my mind getting pregnant was a matter of osmosis — which we had just studied in ninth grade science — except that people, unlike carrots and other vegetables, had to be asleep to osmose.)

"Miss Alice!" It was Emma, the Turners' maid, stopping in her tracks on the sidewalk, turning in at our walk, using her umbrella as a cane. The maids, coming to work from The Hill where the colored people lived to the houses up north where the white folks lived, walked in the opposite direction from the white people going to work in the offices and stores along Main Street. In the heat of summer they strolled under the shade of their umbrellas, heads high and smiling, as though promenading along a boulevard; in the cold of winter or in the rain, carrying the same umbrellas, they hurried along, unseeing, heads down.

Mother held out her peach-wet hands; undeterred, Emma took them in hers and patted them. "The praise be His!" she said. "We spoke to Him 'bout you, Miss Alice."

"Bless you, Emma," Mother said, wiping the peach juice from Emma's hands with a dish towel.

"He have somethin' in mind fer you, that's why He save you."

Yes, I thought. Yes indeed. *Me*. Me and how I need her.

When Mother and Nanna had driven away this spring to the Scott-White clinic down in Texas, they had left me with one of Mother's friends. As the days passed into weeks, the spring into summer, I was shunted from one friend to another, a perennial houseguest, threatening at any moment to become a resident orphan. In this game of musical chairs, the loser would be the one with me under her roof when the music stopped.

Then one day the music did falter. A call came from Nanna, down in Texas, saying that Mother was not expected to live through the night. The message was relayed, secondhand, to me. In a bare statement of fact. A mere string of words — like captions under empty frames. All that I could make of them was that somewhere, three hundred miles away, in a town I'd never heard of and could not picture, in a hospital I'd never seen, my mother — lying on institutional sheets — was absorbed in a battle I could not imagine.

Unable to fill out the blankness of whatever was happening down in that hospital in the here-and-now, I spent the hours of that day urgently gleaning from memory the fading pictures from the past and fending off those of the future. But, unbidden, they kept intruding — scenes with blotted-out spaces where I should have been: of me, invisible, making my way along the corridors of my high school years, making my way down the aisle in the graduation procession. Invisible. Because the only eyes that mattered to me had done with the business of watching and caring.

Now, with Mother home again, with Mrs. Davis pumping her wheezy joy up and down the block, with me the cynosure of Mother's eyes and she of mine, I felt beyond the reach of mortal hurts.

Of all who turned in at our walk and climbed our steps that morning, none gave Mother so much pleasure as Ted Wheeler in his striped overalls and brand new, wide-brimmed farmer's hat. Ted — who made his living pedalling around town on a bicycle-cart, selling ice cream in the summer and tamales in the winter — was epileptic and simple-minded. On his continual rounds, ringing his bell and waving to everyone (whether he knew them or not), he was as much a part of the local landscape as the courthouse. He knew Mother's name, it turned out, called her "Miss Alice," as the colored maids did, grinned and nodded, grinned and nodded, each nod seeming to say, "Yes, isn't this fine," seeming to say "Yes, even I, simple Ted, can recognize a miracle when I see one."

Happiness was not the only gift the summer brought to me. Worldly wisdom was another. It began with the afternoon callers.

These callers, unlike the townspeople on their way to work, arrived by design and not by happenstance. Mother's friends — from childhood, from her bridge club, her garden club — came by car, dressed in stylish linen suits and shantung dresses, bearing gifts of cologne, of talcum. And something called a bed jacket, all lace and chiffon. The likes of which Jean Harlow might wear, lying languid on a bed of white satin.

With these callers the jay reached new heights of intimidation; Nanna, new depths of ungraciousness. She was especially peevish about the wispy bed jacket.

At some point in the course of these afternoon visits, Mother would dismiss me with: "Why don't you play the new *Showboat* records for us?" or "Have you started Jane Austen yet?" (She was easing me away from damsels in distress.)

In the dim light of the library (kept in a perpetual gloom by the big front porch) I'd pull the chain on the floor lamp, watch the flowers of its fringed shade emerge — dewed with crystal beads — then turning to the walnut panatrope, I'd find the record, place it on the turntable, insert a fresh needle in the playing arm, and wind the crank on the side of the cabinet.

Across the room at the oak bookcases, I'd open the leaded-glass doors, pause wistfully at *When Knighthood Was In Flower,* then pick up *Pride and Prejudice,* carry it over to the big, scratchy, mohair-plush chair, and there I'd sit, in my hand the gentle realities of Jane Austen, in my head the romantic configurations of legend and myth, while in through the open window drifted the raw, unpatterned data of Dixter life.

"Two years now," Clara Dotson was saying. Clara and Mother, both in their early thirties, had grown up together over on the east side of Hog Wallow Creek (the creek that divided Dixter as decisively as railroad tracks divide other towns). They still shared jokes about nighttime treks to the privy — slugging through the mud or slipping on the ice, the wind blowing their skirts and their long pigtails, and the lightning making scary shadows. To Clara everything was the stuff of jokes; I had never seen her cross and never seen her mopey. But now her voice, coming through the open window, mingling with the strains of "Make Believe," sounded troubled.

She was talking about her husband. "Two years . . . just sitting round the house." It was true; every time I'd been to Clara's, he was sitting in the chair by the dried pampas grasses, a newspaper in his lap. A handsome man, with clear dark skin, black hair, eyes so black the pupils seemed to have devoured their irises. "Foreign-looking" was the way Dixter described him.

"It unmans him," she said.

"Another Depression eunuch," Mother said. "Not the only one, I hear." (I tried several spellings of "eunuch" in the dictionary before giving up, learning no more than I had known before.)

"He's gotten to imagining things — jealous things," Clara's voice choked off, then resumed. "Even about Eddie." (Clara worked, part-time, at Eddie's Flower Shoppe.)

Mother laughed. "Poor sissy Eddie. Wouldn't he be flattered!"

Then there was pretty Maybelle Jackson, looking like Mary Pickford, with her marcelled hair and her little-girl mouth. But for all her childlike prettiness, she was tough enough to outwait Nanna's withering welcome, to chatter pointlessly, unflustered and unhurried, until Nanna — who had no knack for speaking trivia — retreated, furious, into the house.

Before long, Maybelle, like Clara, was choking up —

something about her husband and someone named Ann
Marie.

A different sort of caller was the Baptist preacher's
wife ("poor mousey Ellen," Nanna called her) who,
always thoughtful, telephoned first. In preparation,
Nanna and I made iced tea and set up a tray.

As we were carrying the tray and glasses and pitcher
through the library and entry hall, we saw — coming
confidently up the porch steps — a woman in a wide-
brimmed hat, a sunback dress, and barefoot sandals. (In
Dixter sunback dresses were acceptable only on young
girls, preferably girls whose breasts had not yet
blossomed.)

"Another one," muttered Nanna, "coming to dump
her sniveling troubles on your poor Mother." Stopping in
her tracks, she plopped the tray down on the hall table
and headed toward the screen door, ready to do battle.

I remained in the back of the hallway, wincing for this
unsuspecting well-wisher.

"Why, Ellen! I didn't recognize you!" I heard Mother
saying.

Without even turning around, Nanna wheeled
around, back into the hall, plopped the tray down on the
hall table.

"What have you done to yourself?" Mother asked.

"Same as you," she answered. "Hauled myself back from the dead." She crossed the porch and took Mother's good arm in her hands.

"I didn't know," Mother said.

"Of course you didn't. We've been . . . away, you and I."

Nanna picked up the tray again.

"Except I made it back with both breasts — though I'm missing a few other parts."

I could hear her, pulling a rocker across the porch, saying, "So here we are. Two Lazaruses."

Nanna, tray in hand, headed out the screen door. I followed. Out on the porch she stood boldly, unblinkingly, studying the face she always said had put her in mind of corn meal mush, the face that now — painted and pencilled — smiled up at her. The mascaraed eyes — that once had wandered, dull and unfocused, as though they had lost both interest and hope — returned Nanna's bold stare.

Finally, pronouncing her judgment, Nanna said, "Whatever you got down with, you should've got it sooner." After putting the tray on the coping and motioning me to start serving, she sat down across from

Ellen and continued her appraisal, from the painted toenails to the arched eyebrows. "You've shaved your legs," she announced.

"Yes . . ." Ellen ran her hand down the back of one leg, ". . . virgin hair, too."

"What got into you?" Though not one for small talk, Nanna was never one for circumspection.

Still looking straight into Nanna's eyes, she answered, "The Devil. At least that's what Edwin said." (Edwin was her husband — Reverend Jenkins).

"You should invite him back," Nanna replied. Shaving your legs, wearing makeup, even painting your toenails — these were what Nanna called "church peoples' sins" — nothing to do with God.

"He won't come near me anymore," Ellen said.

"Edwin or the Devil?" Mother asked.

They began to laugh, all three of them. I poured the iced tea and passed the sugar and lemon. I poured none for myself. My cup was already running over.

After the sun went down, after the supper dishes were washed, after Nanna went to her room to get out of her girdle, Mother and I returned to the cool of the porch.

Rocking away, with no sound but the creaking of our chairs and the occasional antiphony of a few crickets, we sat in the dark, watching old crippled Ned moving about in his small room behind the Simses' garage, watching Mrs. Sims and her pregnant daughter washing the supper dishes, watching the miraculously conceived children running from the dining room to the kitchen and back again, disappearing into rooms beyond our vantage point.

"Let's talk about babies," Mother began. As her story got going, with the crickets like wise old aunts making admonitory comments, I was grateful for the dark of the porch. But mostly I was grateful to learn there was no danger in falling asleep on bus trips.

All at once she changed the subject. (I had long since learned that behind Mother's apparent discontinuities lay hidden links, some logical, some conjectural, some purely imaginative.) "There's nothing so funny as tragedy," she said.

I waited.

"Take the story of that Sims girl. A girl that no one ever took any notice of. And when someone did, she became the joke of the town. Tell it anywhere — it brings the house down."

Across the street in the Simses' house, the downstairs lights went off; the upstairs lights came on. The crickets, no longer confining themselves to an occasional bit of repartee, became downright clamorous.

"Bet they're arguing over how many angels can stand on the head of a pin," Mother commented. We listened.

"Or take poor Ellen Jenkins's story," (are we going back to tragedy — I wondered — or to babies?) "with that pious husband of hers telling it around that she's been possessed by the Devil — and that now the Devil's after *his* soul."

I laughed. Even I, who could fancy a stray fairy here and there, didn't believe in devils.

"Just because she has taken interest in life, now that life has lost interest in her," Mother said.

"But the *Devil?*" I sniggered.

"Yes, very funny. Except that it's dead serious. And, therefore, very sad."

Then, Mother seemed to have wandered again. "A deer. Ensnared in a dark forest. With night coming on."

Returning, she got up from her rocker, her voice brisk again. "Tomorrow we'll read about a magic forest where the queen of the fairies pines away for a jackass, and we can think about pretty Maybelle, pining away . . . and we can laugh and laugh." As she passed behind my chair, she reached over with her good arm, lifted my head, snuggled her face in my hair. "What a busy day we'll have."

And we did. We started *Midsummer Night's Dream;* we planned a picnic for my friends — making the menu and the grocery list, multiplying the recipe by the appetites; we went together to choose a dress pattern for her to use in teaching me to sew; and all the while she talked — telling me about witch-burning in the Middle Ages and about the Scopes trial and all the hullabaloo and hatred it let loose . . . What we could not do that day we postponed to the next. All that summer, it was as though I were going off to make my way in life and she was packing everything I would need — a few social graces, a few friends, a few practical skills, a few windows onto beauty, and over all of these, a tonic dash of heresy.

And the days were so full and so happy that I failed to wonder about the sense of urgency — except to think that she was concerned about my backwardness.

As for Nanna, with every new crop that appeared at the farmers' vegetable stands, she put us through a purgatory of canning. There we'd be, with the thermometer — even in the shade of the back porch — reading 105 degrees, with Nanna standing at the cook stove like Casey Jones at the throttle, keeping all four burners going full blast, their blue-bright flames sending the thermometer higher — and higher — while the clouds of steam rising from the sterilizing kettles fogged Nanna's glasses, frizzed the natural curl of Mother's hair, straightened the hard-come-by curl of mine.

Yet, when it came to my picnic or to Mother's reading aloud with me, Nanna would scold, "Alice, you're doing too much."

Mostly, Mother would set her mouth and go on with what she was doing, but once, when she was planning to drive me and three friends to Medicine Park, forty miles away, she turned on Nanna with, "For God's sake, Mama, do you think it'll make any difference what I do or don't do?"

So, while the vines on the porch grew fuller and less lacy, while the baby jays left their nest and their mother left off her fretting, I learned about comedy and tragedy, original sin and Darwin, pinking shears and French seams.

And I learned that boys can be special. Being too young to date, we grew adept at social improvisation — that is, at organizing pretexts for getting together. From porch parties to storytelling hour at the poor house. Four of us, a particular four, even came up with a long-range, ongoing pretext: a skit for a homeroom program the ensuing year.

As our skit had to have, perforce, four parts, I suggested the "Pyramus and Thisbe" playlet from *Midsummer Night's Dream* (forgetting the fifth role, Moonshine). And because no one else had any other idea, the others went along.

As it was now that time of summer when people in Dixter fled from the heat of their houses as soon as the sun went down, we held our rehearsals out in the side yard, between our house and the First Baptist Church — any night but Sunday and Wednesday, when our voices could not compete with the hymn-singing of The Saved.

During our first run-through, we thought ourselves hilarious. During the second, all palled. As we were voicing our doubts about our choice, Mother came out from the porch to check the watermelon we were icing down in the washtub.

"The trouble is, you're playing it like a comedy," she said.

After a polite silence, Buzz Lawson said, "Well, I guess so!"

"But it's not funny," Mother said.

"Yeah. But it *was,* the first time," Buzz argued.

"No. I mean, not to the characters. To them it's tragedy."

"Oh . . ."

"Think of it as *Romeo and Juliet.*" (She had taken us to the movie with Norma Shearer and Leslie Howard.) "It isn't so far from Romeo's 'Eyes, look your last' to Pyramus's 'Eyes, do you see?'"

Pulling her hands from the ice water and wiping them on a napkin she said, "Play it straight, like a tragedy. But, first, reverse the casting."

So, big, lumbering, orange-eyed Buzz Lawson, who'd been playing the Lion, became the heroine; and sweet-voiced Mary Lee Hopkins, who'd been playing the heroine, became the Lion; while cocky Wayne Moyer became Wall, and I, the most timorous of the group, the bumptious Bottom.

First, there was the matter of the watermelon. While Buzz wrestled it out of the icy water, Wayne and Mary Lee and I went into the house to bring out the bridge table and chairs, plates, and forks. Then, after we had eaten, and after Buzz and Wayne had a seed spitting contest, we went back to "Pyramus and Thisbe."

Because we had overlooked getting someone to play Moonshine, we asked Mother to fill in. For her lantern we gave her a flashlight; for her dog, my teddy bear; and, to place her up in the sky where all good moons belong, we brought a ladder from the garage. Wayne, looking up at her standing above us, with her flashlight held aloft, told her she looked like the Statue of Liberty.

Just as we were getting into our lines, Nanna's voice, calling from the porch, announced that a storm was coming. We stopped, listened: not so much as a breeze or a rumbling. We searched the sky: nothing but an occasional greenish-blue glow in the southwest. We went back to our lines.

Nanna — who as a young woman, pregnant with Mother, had emerged from the storm cellar after a tornado to find her house sitting drunkenly out in the pasture — didn't mess around with storms. She was already inside the house, noisily closing windows.

After a while the intermittent glow changed to bright flashes, came closer, 'till we could hear the thunder, soft and grumbly. Then we heard a rustling from the catalpa leaves along the street and, next, felt on our faces the breeze that had stirred them. Big blobs of rain began to fall. Just a few — but big. Nanna called from a window,

saying we must collect the chairs and tables and dishes —
right now. Knowing Mother didn't like Nanna bossing
her around like a child, I turned to read her face, to see
whether we should oblige. She was still on the ladder,
still holding the torch — high. With every flash of
lightning, her face would appear up there in the night —
distinct, white, ghostly — only to dissolve again into the
dark, exactly the way the moon itself appears from
behind a passing cloud, only to be eclipsed by still
another.

As I stood there, looking at her, the blobs of rain
changed to real rain, steady and blowing, the flashes of
lightning to blue and jagged streaks, and the soft thunder
turned malevolent — cracking and booming and threatening. Mary Lee Hopkins gave out a sweet shriek. Nanna
exhorted, unheard, from a window. Wayne and Buzz
folded the table and grabbed the chairs, while Mary Lee

tried simultaneously and unsuccessfully to gather up the
plates and to cover her hair. I looked again at Mother,
and there she stood, still on the ladder, watching with
charmed attention as the wind whipped the branches of
the trees like posies in a nosegay, lifting her face straight
into the rain, smiling at the barking sky, as though, in all
her years in storm-ridden Oklahoma, she had never

before been so privileged as to witness a real storm.

Her hair was dripping and still she did not move.

"Alice! What do you think you're doing? You . . ." Nanna's voice was lost in a sudden rolling of booms.

Mother climbed down, picked up a wet napkin from the grass, reached out her free hand to mine, and said, "I suppose it's . . . time."

We were well into winter before it came our turn to perform at school. The Virginia creeper vines that had curtained the porch had long since turned brown and blown away, exposing the nest we had known was there but had never seen.

Wayne Moyer explained to the class that we were going to perform the Shakespearean tragedy, "Pyramus and Thisbe." Then Buzz Lawson came in, wearing on his head, like a wedding veil, a white chiffon scarf. Everything was going along just as we hoped, with us remembering our lines and our business, with the class laughing at all the right places — until I came to the lines, "Sweet Moon, I thank thee for thy sunny beams; / I thank thee, Moon, for shining now so bright."

I was looking at Frieda Lambert, standing on a chair

with a flashlight in one hand and my teddy bear in the other, and all at once I knew I was in trouble. My eyes were beginning to fill, and Frieda was becoming a wobbly blur. At "shining now so bright," my voice staged a mutiny all its own. By the time I pulled my cardboard sword to slay myself, I had more tears than voice.

But no matter — the class was so beside itself with laughter, they wouldn't have heard the lines anyway. Even Mrs. Barnes, our teacher, who seldom managed more than a sick smirk, let go with a chuckle.

When the play was ended and the uproar had tapered off, she said, "Well . . . I hope Betty Jane never tries to play a *real* tragedy."

I wanted to tell her about comedy and tragedy, but I didn't. Just as I had not contradicted Reverend Jenkins when earlier in the winter he had admonished me that Christians should grieve only at births, not at deaths.

Not that I was crying at the time. I hadn't cried at all.

That morning, very early, in my bedroom upstairs off by itself, I'd awakened to Nanna's voice, beside me and over me, loud, abrupt.

"Get up, Betty Jane."

I opened my eyes. She was turning away, heading back toward the door of the room.

"Get dressed. Your mother's dying."

Having delivered herself of this summons, she was gone.

Fumbling my way into the clothes I'd taken off the night before, I found the snaps of my dress placket suddenly unfamiliar and unmanageable. Leaving it gaping open, I went downstairs, through the back hall, where I could see clusters of people coming into the library and into the entrance hall. Holding my placket together, I headed for Mother's room; Nanna was nowhere to be seen.

The nurse, who had come a few days earlier, was standing beside Mother's bed, reaching for the sheet. Mother was lying in the bed, propped up on pillows, her eyes open, her mouth hanging open. I went over and kneeled down close beside her head, reached for one of her hands, and began talking to her. "Mother . . ." Then someone's strong hands on my shoulder were pulling me up, pulling me away. The nurse, firmly, was leading me, pushing me from the room. In the doorway, looking in, stood Clara Dotson and Maybelle Jackson, their faces red with crying. Out in the hall were other faces I knew vaguely, out of some other life, these faces, too, wet with crying. Mine was dry. The nurse's hand on

93

my shoulders kept pushing me through the people gathered there in the hall. I heard Clara saying, "Take her to the kitchen," and someone else, ". . . and her mother already dead. Someone should have told the child."

On through the pantry I was ushered, through the breakfast room, and into the kitchen. There, fat Mrs. Sims, talking to two church ladies, cracking an egg into a skillet, said, "Come what may, child, we must eat." I saw Nanna, out in the hall, talking to two men in black suits.

Nudging me with all her three hundred pounds, Mrs. Sims got me to the pine table and put the fried egg and toast in front of me. I sat, dutifully, staring at it, my throat full. After what I deemed a decent length of time, I got up and went out into the dining room. It, too, had filled with people I scarcely knew, except for someone over on the other side of the room, someone who looked like the ghost of Ellen Jenkins. I wandered through, directionless, seemingly invisible, for no one spoke. Indeed, they looked away as I passed. On into the living room I drifted, where Clara Dotson came up and said I should go to Nanna in the library.

Over by the window in the big, mohair-plush chair, where I had read Jane Austen the summer before, Nanna was accepting someone's muttered sympathy; seeing me, she motioned for me to come over. I did. She motioned that I should stand there, beside her. And I did. Like an attendant page, just the way I had stood beside Mother out on the big front porch when she was receiving the passersby.

That time, Nanna had not been gracious. This time, she was — as near as she knew how — receiving the undertaker, the church ladies, Mother's friends, giving no offense, bowing her head almost humbly when Reverend Jenkins got down on one knee in front of us and began praying. She even kept her peace when he said how God moves in mysterious ways, His wonders to perform — though I saw her right foot begin to tap.

But when he started telling God how lucky we were, having His promise of a second chance, she raised her head, opened her eyes and glared straight out at his bowed head.

"Reverend Jenkins . . ." she intoned.

He stopped and looked around him, as though unsure whose voice had invoked his name.

"Maybe you can explain to me," she said, "those mysterious ways."

I grew apprehensive. "What will she say next?" I

wondered. As for Reverend Jenkins, he was clearly nonplussed.

"I'll tell you straight," she continued, "the way I see it, it's God who needs a second chance."

All through that day and the next I stood there beside Nanna's chair, mute, invisible, a mere stage prop, while people came and went, while the wreaths and sprays gradually filled the room. Mother, also mute, lay now in the living room, surrounded at last with the accoutrements appropriate to a sleeping princess, dressed no longer in gingham but in dusty rose lace, lying on a bed of white satin.

She, unseeing; me, unseen: it would have been unsuitable to have cried.

Yet my not crying became the only thing I did — rather didn't do — that became visible. ". . . and she never shed a tear," they said. From Nanna, I was not to hear the end of it. Ever.

In spite of what they said or Nanna said or Reverend Jenkins said or Mrs. Barnes said, I knew perfectly well when to cry and when to laugh — knew far better than all the people who laughed about the Sims girl. Mother had taught me all that.

She even taught me what to expect — because when I did cry, when I was looking up at Frieda Lambert playing Moonshine and all the while remembering Mother's face appearing in the lightning, dissolving in the rain, and when the tears came at last, wracking and unquenchable, it was just the way Mother said it was when someone finally took note of the Sims girl: it brought the house down.

THE SILVER
DESOTO

THE FIRST SIGN CAME in Miss Hesselbach's Plane Geometry class, when I looked up and saw Mary Jo Keene coming toward me down the aisle, looking straight at me, smiling. It had to mean I had become visible again.

The problem started after Mother died. When I came back to school the Monday after the funeral, everyone managed to be looking the other way when I walked by. I understood. I had become an embarrassment. Someone they didn't know how to deal with.

Now here was Mary Jo, who was about as visible as anyone you'd ever find (can't take my eyes off her, people would say), inviting me to a party.

"Bring a date," she was saying, smiling at me almost the way she smiled at boys. *Some* boys, that is.

"I don't date," I replied. I was only fourteen — two

years younger than the others in my class, and Nanna didn't let me have dates yet.

"What about Bob Wyant?" She seemed to be accusing me of something.

"What about him?"

"You think we haven't *seen* you?" she allowed one corner of her pretty mouth to curl ever so slightly.

"Seen what?"

"Forget it." She walked on past me, back to her own seat.

I supposed the invitation was withdrawn. Even so, I was encouraged, knowing they were allowing themselves to see me again. When I was with Bob, anyway. (Bob Wyant, by common consent, was the handsomest boy in Dixter High School.)

The first time Bob had come by for me was the night after Mother's funeral. When the doorbell rang and I went to open the door, I expected to see one of the church ladies who had been so good about bringing us food but so bad about always saying, "Your mother's better off, where she is now," making me feel selfish, as though I were grieving about what happened to me rather than about what happened to her.

But it wasn't a church lady, there at the door. It was Bob Wyant, smiling that brown-eyed smile of his.

"Wanna go for a ride?"

Out behind him, parked at the curb, looking as though it had just landed, was his father's brand new, streamlined, silver DeSoto, the first streamlined car ever to ride the streets of Dixter. All the other cars were the stubby, hit-the-air-head-on kind, with headlights and radiators and windshields that just slammed square up against the wall of the air; but the silver DeSoto was all bulbous and curvy, with billowy fenders and fat balloon tires, like a fat possum that could just nuzzle its way along, as easy as into downy comforts.

Nanna said yes I could go for a ride. *She* understood it wasn't a date, even if no one in school did.

Bob's parents (Russ and Norma Wyant) had been among those friends of Mother's who took turns keeping me, the weeks when she was in the Scott-White Hospital down in Texas. It was while I was staying at their house that the early morning call came from Nanna: the doctors didn't expect Mother to make it through another night. And it was Russ and Norma who decided it wasn't right that I should have to wander around their house all day, waiting, with no one to talk to but this family I scarcely knew.

"Betty Jane," Norma found me in their shade-drawn living room, where I had gone after the call so no one would see me crying. "Russ and I are going to drive you down there. So you run and pack, honey." Then, as she turned to leave, "Need any help?"

"No, ma'am."

I did wish, though, that I had a summer dress. Or a clean skirt. No one I'd stayed with had thought to ask about those same three winter, wool skirts I'd been wearing all these weeks; unlike the blouses — which I kept washed and ironed — the skirts had to go to the dry cleaners, and I had no money. Besides, with the temperature now reaching the nineties every day, they were hot and scratchy.

Within an hour and a half after Nanna's call, Russ had arranged for someone to take his place at the oil rig, Norma had arranged for Bob to stay with a friend, and Russ, Norma, and I, in their big black La Salle, were out on the highway, headed south. Toward that hospital three hundred miles away.

After we got there, Russ and Norma took rooms in the

same white frame rooming house with Nanna and me, took turns sitting with Mother while Nanna and I ate. Not until the third day, when Mother was judged to be out of danger, did they speak of returning home. I was to stay a few days longer, then return by bus.

This time, unlike the rushed departure from Dixter, Norma had the landlady make sandwiches to take along, and Russ left the La Salle all day for a check-up — even had it washed and waxed.

Early the following morning, just as the sun slipped loose from the horizon and turned the windows of the hospital into bright pink mirrors, Nanna and I stood on the curb in front of the rooming house and waved goodbye as the big black La Salle, all bright and clean, drove away. Norma, leaning out the window, waving, called, "See you at the bus station!"

But when I got off the bus, I was met by Clara Dotson (another of Mother's friends). Not that I was surprised. Or disappointed. Or even curious. I had grown accustomed to being shunted from one friend to another, one house to another. So, unquestioning, I got into Clara's car, carrying the suitcase containing my three wool skirts and cotton blouses.

Not until three days later did Clara tell me about it. We were sitting together in their wooden swing under the honeysuckle arbor, waiting for an evening breeze. Having had a letter from Nanna saying she and Mother were coming home the next week, I was happy, smelling the heavy sweetness of the honeysuckle, joking with Clara about the noisy locusts.

Then she told me.

I didn't cry. Being alone with my feelings all those weeks, I had lost the knack of showing them.

I remember wanting to scream at the locusts — make them shut up. I even remember thinking the world must be run by locusts. And I remember especially thinking of Mother, lying in that hospital, vulnerable to every vagrant whim of some uncaring power.

"Tell me how it happened," I said.

"A drunk, coming out of a roadhouse," she said, then added, in disbelief that anyone should be getting drunk in a roadhouse in broad daylight, "right in the middle of the day."

The locusts, louder than ever, continued their raucous mocking.

"Just this side of Waco." She told me the story as she

had heard it from others and as they had heard it from Russ.

The La Salle, hit from the side, rolled over and over — Russ wasn't sure how many times — into the ditch, out the other side, across a barbed-wire fence, coming to rest upside-down in a field, its front wheels still spinning.

The people who stopped found Russ, pinned by one leg, thrashing about like an animal in a trap, calling out, "Where is my wife? Find my wife."

Because, as he could see, Norma wasn't inside the car. On one of those rolls, as nearly as anyone could piece together, she must have been thrown clear. When they found her, she was lying in a field of Texas bluebonnets, the very bluebonnets, Russ would recall and recount over and over, that only moments before she had called to his attention.

The drunk, staggering from one to another of the people who stopped to help, kept assuring them, "I got insurance, you understand, plenty of insurance."

"When can you take me to see Russ?" I asked.

"That's no place for you; you're too young." The way she said it made it sound like the notion was totally inappropriate. "You'd just be in the way."

As I was inured to being in the way, I insisted. So the next afternoon, she drove me over. "I'll pick you up at the library," she said as I was getting out of the car. (The library had served as one of my surrogate mothers that spring and summer.)

So when I rang the doorbell, I was alone. Wondering how to apologize for being alive and well — and unbereft.

Something I didn't learn until several days later was that the uncle who drove Bob down to Waco didn't tell him until just outside the town that they were not headed for the Waco hospital but for the undertaker's parlor. I tried to imagine what the uncle had talked about, all those five long deceitful hours.

After Norma's funeral Bob had become invisible to everyone but grown-ups. And to me.

The La Salle, crumpled like a discarded letter, ended up in a Texas junk yard. That's how it happened that, right in the middle of the Depression, Russ bought a brand new car. The silver DeSoto. And that's why Bob's taking me for rides in it had nothing to do with his being a boyfriend.

Not that he wouldn't have qualified, with that wide, clear forehead of his and the thick brown hair, and the strong chin. But most of all with those smiling brown eyes. Oh yes, when I would answer the doorbell and see him standing there, grinning that brown-eyed grin, and see the silver DeSoto out at the curb, waiting, and hear him asking, "Wanna go for a ride?" I could easily have cast him as Prince Charming — coach and all. But, fated as he and I were, we had already been cast as Hansel and Gretel.

At school I enjoyed being visible again. Being invited to parties. Though with that invariable proviso, "Bring a date." Prompting my invariable reply, "I don't date," and their "What do you call it then?" and my "Call what?" and their "Running around at night in that fancy car with Bob Wyant."

So it was a standoff — them drawing their own conclusions, me not knowing how to explain, the girls deciding I was just too jealous to let Bob loose among them, the boys deciding we were just "a couple of spooks."

Either way, the invitations were no longer extended.

Maybe the boys were right, calling us spooks. We were like those ghosts you read about, who no longer belong anywhere, who — unconsolable and invisible — haunt familiar rooms, frighten old friends.

While Bob and I were being initiated into the rites of death, our classmates were being initiated into Dixter's rites of adolescence. They had learned about bunching into booths at Henry's Hot Dogs, about the protocol of grouping and regrouping, like dancers in a pattern, out in front of Coleman's Drug Store, while you waited, double parked, for the carhop to bring your order. They had learned that on a regular date a boy had only a dime to spend, and that for a dime both of you could get a Coke or a Dr. Pepper, or small limeade, cherry Coke, vanilla Coke, lemon Coke, Coke-limeade, frozen malt cone, single-dip cone, or a small chocolate sundae. They also had learned that on a dance date a boy had a quarter and you could suggest going to Henry's for a coney island. And that movie dates, costing more, meant a girl was rather special.

Knowing none of these techniques — and being invisible anyway — Bob and I would ride out on scouting expeditions where, from the security of the DeSoto, we could study the goings-on of our peers.

"Like Marco Polo, ogling the Orientals," Bob said one night as we eased along by the Elks Club, driving so slow the DeSoto stalled. We were watching the silhouettes of couples as they danced by the tall windows, swaying, melding, dividing, like organisms swimming under a microscope.

Rousing myself to answer, I said, "More like Flash Gordon — in his sleek new airship."

Eventually that was the way we thought of ourselves and our nighttime rides — as alien creatures flying in from another planet, hovering low in our silver ship, fascinated by the ways of the natives.

Toward the end of the school year Nanna decided she needed to get away. In Dixter in those days, *away* meant out of the heat. Which meant Colorado Springs.

After driving out as paying passengers with the Howard sisters (who though long since married and even widowed, were still referred to as the Howard sisters), we rented two dark rooms that smelled like the old man who rented them to us — who lived in the rest of the rooms.

What this man did with his days I never knew, except that he must have spent a lot of time just standing around in the hallway listening to us, because every time I came out of our door, there he was, and he would come up to me, close and smelly, and start telling me how I should never let myself be a "bad girl" — and all the while that he talked, he would be looking at my breasts.

Through all the endless weeks of that summer neither our routine nor our meals ever varied. For breakfast we ate Rocky Ford cantaloupe and toast, for dinner Rocky Ford cantaloupe and corn on the cob. Every morning we walked to a shopping area that had several antique stores (where Nanna looked but never bought), then we would buy an ice cream cone for our lunch, walk back to our rooms, where Nanna would nap and I would read or walk to the library for a new book. After her nap we would walk to the city park (and always on these walks Nanna's shoelaces would come untied and I would have to squat down on the sidewalk and tie them because she was all girdled up for the day). At the park we would sit on the benches beside the old ladies and the old men, and the old ladies would tell sad tales of fair and flawless daughters, of tall and loving sons — now gone. Or dead. Nanna, in her turn, in her telling, would transform the

112

misery of her life into a golden tale.

And thus the days went by.

But I had secret walks of my own. I walked the moors of *Wuthering Heights* with Heathcliff; I walked the dark passageways of Thornfield Hall, waiting for a Rochester to round the corner. The passionate sufferings of those abandoned children, it seemed to me, were far to be preferred to the blankness of mine.

One night, as I was sitting in our reeking rooms, reading *Tess of the D'Urbervilles,* our landlord knocked on our door.

"A young man to see you," he said, looking down at my breasts.

"Me?" I asked. "You sure?" I didn't know anyone in Colorado Springs — except the Howard sisters.

"Mmm — " he frowned.

Deciding it must be the paper boy, collecting, I got money from Nanna, went down the hall, into the entrance way — and there, in the doorway, stood Bob Wyant, smiling that brown-eyed smile of his. Out behind him at the curb, waiting, was the silver DeSoto — for a minute I almost thought it had flown him here.

"Wanna go for a ride?" he said, proud of himself.

"Yes!" I whirled around, ran back down the hall to tell

Nanna where I was going.

Out in the car, we just sat there, grinning, until it occurred to me to ask, "How did you get here?"

"Dad's been going out with a woman who lives here."

"Oh." So Bob was supposed to make himself invisible.

"Been to the Garden of the Gods?" he asked.

"Of course not," I replied.

He started the car, turned on the lights, and off we went. Out to explore the universe.

Not knowing our way, we just followed the broadest streets, checking our direction against the silhouette of the Sangre de Cristo mountains off to the west, a black bulk against the cobwebby clouds of a moon-bright night. We drove past houses with amber windows, houses unlike any in Dixter — steep-roofed, many-gabled houses, turreted and towered houses, houses with stained glass entries that threw their colored pictures out across the porches, houses that had been reaching their pointed roofs into the Colorado sky when Dixter was still a trading settlement in Indian Territory.

Coming to a street lighted up like the midway at the county fair, where the whole night sky seemed to be spattered with jewels, we turned down it, to investigate. We found three movie houses, an ice cream parlor, and a

114

miniature golf course. Continuing on, we saw again, up ahead of us, our compass — the silhouette of the mountains. Following it, we turned onto a road spangled with neon animals — red rabbits, pink elephants, green cats — and with lots of long-stemmed neon cocktail glasses. And long-stemmed neon waitresses.

"The humanoids here must drink a lot," Bob said.

We hadn't said much, but that was nothing new, for neither to Bob nor to me had words ever been easy. Yet our silences had never been awkward or embarrassing, being always as much a part of our gawking and wondering as were any words we ever spoke.

As the restaurants and roadhouses trailed off, the world grew dim, with only the moth-foggy haze of a single bulb in a few empty gas stations. On a dirt road now, the mountains looming closer and bigger, the dark was broken only by the headlights of the DeSoto and an occasional orange glow from a window, from a few distant houses. The last outposts.

Soon, off in the distance to the left, we saw a great dark blotch, without a single light. Just an emptiness. A black nothingness. At the next crossroad, Bob turned toward it. We passed a last house, with its single, glowing window, went over a rise, and now there was just us and the darkness and the headlights of the DeSoto.

What the headlights revealed was no more than a few unprepossessing foothills.

"Think we should try another planet?" Bob asked.

Before I could say anything, we came to the top of a ridge — and saw the answer.

While Bob and I stared, stunned and silent, the silver DeSoto floated down from the ridge as if coming in for a landing. Bob, reaching out his hand, switched off the headlights, frowned, reached out his hand again, switched off the lights of the instrument panel. As if the gods had spoken, the darkness vanished. And the garden showed itself to us in the same shimmering light as the gods themselves had seen it — the vestigial light of far-off galactic fires.

"What do you think?" Bob whispered.

"I think — " I stopped, shocked by the loudness of my voice. "I think it has," I went on in a whisper, "suffered a visitation."

"Great!" Bob and I were always generous in judging each other's fictions.

"Maybe by a comet's tail . . ." I was warming to the idea. "A hit-and-run comet."

"Sure melted that skyscraper," he pointed to a pinna-

116

cle of red rock.

"You suppose they had curb service?" I asked. "Or coney islands?"

"No," he said. Then pointing to a giant formation that resembled an elephant, he added, "But they had a great zoo."

We enjoyed our game. We'd had lots of practice, coloring the empty spaces of our Dixter days.

Lowering my voice to a whisper again, I warned, "Now we've done it."

"Done what?"

I indicated a shadow, wandering disconsolate, from one ridgetop to another. A faint, muzzy shadow. Cast by a gauzy cloud. "Waked the gods."

Bob pulled to the edge of the dirt road, turned off the motor, rolled down his window — a dead and heavy stillness tumbled in on us.

I could even hear Bob's breathing — easy, slow, rhythmic. After listening, there in the silence, I found myself feeling a strange compulsion to match my breathing to his. And I felt something I'd never felt before — an uneasiness with Bob.

"Let's explore," he said, and the sound of his door, opening and slamming, was like a blasphemy.

Softly, I opened my door and stepped out, leaving it ajar.

Out among the ruins of whatever Armageddon the place had suffered, we picked our way, with the shadows from the clouds running ahead of us, giving warning. Scuffing our feet in the astral dust of our imaginings, we christened each ruin, each fossil: a pillar of the temple, the fossil of a mastodon . . . .

Coming to a giant, other-worldly prairie dog, we sat down at its paws. For a while we said nothing, then, "What if it's not a dead planet, after all?" I ventured.

Knowing the game but not the answer, he waited.

"What if it's a brand new one? Trying to get born?" I stopped, embarrassed, having only a tenuous grasp of what I was thinking — or feeling — and the more I understood of it, the less inclined I was to utter it. What I was reaching for was . . . what if the stillness were the kind just before something happens, before something new is conceived? Nothing to do with dying or with an ending, but something to do with a conception, a beginning?

All I could manage to say was, "What if those shapes are just now . . . beginning to become . . . what if they're . . . just groping . . . toward life?"

118

Bob sat there, saying nothing. Usually, if he didn't take to my fictions, he laughed; he never just left me to feel foolish — like this. Then all at once he jumped up as if an alarm clock had gone off, announcing in a voice loud enough for all of Colorado Springs to hear, "I'd better get you back!"

We started off, up an incline, then I stopped. "Not until we've marked it," I said.

"Marked what?"

"Oh . . . the planet? Like staking our claim to it?" Actually, I was none too sure myself, of just what, or why.

Even though we didn't come up with a good reason for our labors, we worked very hard and for a very long time. All hunched over with the weight, we carried large rocks, placed them on the highest spot around us, stacked them, arranged them, until we achieved something of a puffy, knobby pyramid.

Standing back, admiring it, Bob roared out, "A cairn! That's what it is!"

"Yes!" I shouted.

"All explorers leave a cairn!" Delighted with himself, he picked a twig from a scrubby bush, dubbed it a flag, and wedged it between two of the top rocks. Then, turning suddenly somber, he said, "They also leave them over their dead."

A few days later Bob's father, apparently deciding he had allotted enough time to the business of courtship, drove back to Dixter, taking Bob with him.

When Nanna and I returned, at the end of the summer, I had turned fifteen, and she let me go out on dates. Thus I became qualified for party invitations.

Bob, though two years older and a year ahead of me in school, still did not date and did not accept invitations to parties, for while he had mastered, in the course of our voyages and explorations together, the art of conjuring forth from the unsubstantial air whole histories and towers and domes, he was as yet a novice in the knack of saying nothing, endlessly, in the game of social dalliance.

So it happened that twice that September when he rang our doorbell, I had to tell him I was going out — on a date.

I saw less and less of him.

Soon after the Christmas holidays, the whole high

school began to buzz with the news that Bob Wyant was dating Valerie Dobbs. I told myself I was happy for him.

One night when Phil Hanley picked me up for a movie date, I found when we got to the car that Bob and Valerie were in the back seat. Phil hadn't told me we were double-dating. We went to see *Trail of the Lonesome Pine*, and all through the feature Phil held my hand; then after the movie, in the car driving home, he reached out his arm, pulled me over to him.

The next morning the doorbell rang — and there stood Bob, "Wanna go for a ride?" This was the first time he had ever come by in the day.

No sooner had we driven away from the curb than he said, "I was surprised at you last night."

I laughed, "Well, *I* was surprised at Phil!"

Then he laughed too.

But we never double-dated again.

We did, of course, run into each other, on our dates. Out in front of Coleman's Drug Store. At Henry's for a coney island. Like the night Al Moore and I and Mary Jo Keene and Dick Evans were in a booth at Henry's when Bob and Millie Webster walked in together (he had dated several girls since Valerie).

And all at once Mary Jo began to chirp and carry on as

if Millie were bringing in the crown jewels. "Over here!" she called, waving and pushing her bottom into Dick's to make room, ordering him, without so much as a glance his way, "Scoot over!"

For the rest of the evening I had to sit there and watch Mary Jo — who for two hours had been pouting about Heaven-knows-what — as she fizzed and bubbled all over the booth. The worst was when she called to Dick, who was putting two nickels into the nickelodeon, telling him to play "When My Dreamboat Comes Home" and then turned to Bob, smiling cow eyes at him. On *Dick's* nickel!

Bob, on his part, never missed a beat — matched joke for joke with Dick, acknowledged every innuendo of Mary Jo's with a noncommittal smile. He had schooled himself well in the ceremonies of this once-alien sublunary world.

As I watched him a most extraordinary thing happened. I thought my eyes were playing me false: Bob's features seemed to be melting. I looked over at Dick: *his* were perfectly clear; I looked across to another booth, over to the door — all, perfectly clear. Then I looked back at Bob's face: it was just a confused blur, without a single distinguishing feature.

It happened again the next Saturday night. Four of us were double parked out in front of Coleman's Drug Store when, seeing a hand wave from the back of Dick Evans's car, I asked my date, "Who's that?"

"Where?"

"There."

He gave me a puzzled look, "Bob Wyant."

Like an insect who acquires the stripes and colors of the leaves he lives among, Bob had acquired at last the stripes and colors of Dixter's natives. But in doing so, he had become, to me at least, invisible. I tried to be happy for him.

As it had been months since Bob had rung my door-bell, I was surprised one night just a few days before he was to leave for college, to go to the door and find him standing there, looking exactly as he had all those months before, his features all clear and distinct again — the wide forehead, the sharp chin, and the brown smil-ing eyes. Asking the same question, "Wanna go for a ride?"

But everything else was different. Now he opened the door for me as I got in the car. He asked me where I wanted to go. (Always before, the going itself had been enough.)

"Let's just drive," I said.

And so we did. Past Coleman's Drug, waving as we went. Past the Elks Club. But all those marvels and mysteries had given way to the gray certitudes of knowledge, our artless silences to well-rehearsed antiphonies: we had mastered the native patois, were chattering away in it . . . like the earthlings we had become.

But it was a language in which neither of us had anything to say.

"Wanna drop by Jean's?" he asked. She was having an open house for those leaving for college.

"No!" I rejected the idea as if it were castor oil. Then I heard myself saying, "I want to go to another planet."

He didn't answer. He just started some elaborate tinkering with the instrument panel. Good enough for me, I thought.

"Something wrong?" I asked.

"Checking her out," he said, "to make sure she's still up to it." Even in the dim light of the panel, I could see he was smiling.

We drove to Tallisaw, stopped at a root-beer stand, drove down to the train station where a passenger train had just pulled in.

Bob pointed out a strange thing: you couldn't tell — just from the hugging and the crying — who was arriving and who was leaving.

"Take *them,*" he pointed to an elderly man and woman, "holding onto each other like the last life boat was pulling off — with only one of them on it."

The man had just stepped off the train.

Driving back to Dixter, we tried to invent a story to go with the scene.

Stripe by stripe we were shedding our protective coloring, settling again into those easy silences we had once known. When we did speak it was in the language of those countries and planets we had left behind, somewhere, last summer, that country where we had seen so much pain and death, those planets of our imaginings — a language all our own, unfolding word by word, like wings.

After one of our long but comfortable silences, Bob said, "We never did decide, you know."

I looked over at him. "Decide what?"

"What the cairn stood for." This was the first time in the intervening months that either of us had mentioned it.

"A Beginning or an Ending . . ." I started, hoping *he* would finish it.

But he said nothing.

Pulling up to the curb in front of my house, switching off the motor, he put his hand over on mine. "We've been so close, you and I."

Bob had never before touched me — so it felt like a beginning. Like in that picture in my church book where God reached out a finger and touched Adam, and Adam awoke. And that had been the beginning of life.

Taking away his hand, he got out of the car, came around for me, took me to the door, said he'd call me when he came home for Christmas.

Call me — that too was a first.

Before Christmas came around, Bob's father, Russ, married the woman from Colorado, sold his Dixter house, and moved to a house he bought in Denver. Bob, of course, had to go to Colorado for Christmas.

The following spring Nanna had a stroke and died; the next fall I went away to college. So neither Bob nor I had a home to come to in Dixter.

I never saw Bob Wyant again.

I went on, as I suppose he did, exploring, marvelling at the ways of the peoples just beyond the ridge.

But, as no mere Buick or Boeing 707 could ever go so far or as high as the silver DeSoto, I never again managed such other-worldly flights as when Bob and I flew in low over the streets of Dixter, or as when we landed in the Garden of the Gods and, exploring, scuffed our feet in its astral dust — scaring away its gods.

UNCLE TOM'S
DAYBOOK

T HE SUMMER THAT UNCLE TOM came to live with Nanna and me was the summer that Nelson Eddy looked into Jeanette MacDonald's eyes and sang "Ah! Sweet Mystery of Life," and that Dick Powell took Ruby Keeler to Kissing Rock. My fifteenth summer.

Five o'clock in the afternoon. The thermometer, even in the shade of the back porch, reads 106 degrees.

In my bedroom, I unplug the small buzzing fan, move it from the top of the chiffonier to the floor, reach under the bed with the cord, and plug it in again. Then, lying down in front of it, I stack four volumes of *Encyclopedia Americana* on my chest and, slowly, draw in a deep breath. Sharply, I push it out. Tumbling three of the volumes, but not the fourth. I try again — sharper — and again. Twenty times, but not once dislodging that fourth volume.

Reaching under the bed again, I unplug the fan, move it back to the top of the chiffonier; then, standing in front of it, I roll out broad round vowels, mince out short ones, twirl out tongue-twisters.

The warm-up finished, I pick up a high-school textbook that once belonged to my mother — *Dramatic Expression*. Like all her books, its margins are crammed with her notes — the early ones, like this one, bits of girlish but earnest scholarship, the later ones, her conversations with the author — all of them, evidence that *she* never wasted a summer afternoon as I just have, pondering whether to pluck my eyebrows in an arch like Jean Harlow's or in a gentle curve like Jeanette MacDonald's.

In this book, though, she pencilled one note such as even I might write. Set off by itself, centered above the table of contents, it reads: "Remember March 17, 1915."

She was sixteen.

I turn through to Edmund Burke's "Resolutions for Conciliation with the Colonies, March 22, 1775," and, closing my eyes, planting my feet firmly apart, I picture Nelson Eddy, in waistcoat and ruffles and wig, speaking in the House of Commons . . . . Then I begin, "I hope, Sir, that notwithstanding the austerity . . . ." Two paragraphs, then back to the beginning, trying new phrasing, different emphases. The salt sweat runs down my face, stings my eyes, makes me cry mock tears.

I stop, wipe my face, reread her careful notes in the margin, and wonder, "What's the use?"

Even Mother, smart as she was and as much as she studied, ended her days right here in Dixter, right here in this very room, still under my grandmother's thumb. With never a soul to talk to, not about the books anyway. Not even my father, who married her and went looking for oil and came back only for visits. And certainly not the ladies of the Tuesday Bridge Club. Not anyone. Except me.

Me. Of all people. Who, even before I went to school, had practically given up talking. Just stopped, for the most part. No one knew why.

Mother had taken it upon herself to coax words back into me — or out of me.

In this very room. Sitting in that Windsor chair over by the window, with me sitting on the bench of the dressing table. First, she would read to me — a story or a poem. Then, having me stand up, she would go back and

read the first line, then have me repeat it. Word perfect.
Then she would read the second line and have me repeat
the first and add the second to it. Then the third . . .
adding line by inexorable line, until I could recite from
memory Oscar Wilde's "The Selfish Giant" or Poe's "The
Bells" (her, giving no quarter, not even on such words as
tintinnabulation). By the time I learned to read for myself,
I had already memorized a considerable repertoire of
poems and stories.

The idea of the speech lessons had come to Mother
the first time I stopped talking, when I was four. This
next time, when I was in the first grade, she took me out
of school. This is what happened: she had been in the
kitchen, rolling out pie crust, when she looked up and
saw me coming across the back porch toward the
kitchen.

"What are you doing," she asked, "coming home at
this time of day?"

"I have to go to the bathroom."

"Bathroom?" She was not pleased. "Don't they have
bathrooms at school?"

I said nothing, just stood there, holding onto the
doorknob.

"Are you sick?" she asked.

Still, I said nothing.

"Answer me, Betty Jane!"

I tightened my grip on the doorknob.

She tried again. "Don't you know where the bathrooms are?"

She was giving me every excuse — but not the right one.

"Don't just stand there like that!" Now she was losing her patience. But what could I do?

Looking like she was counting to ten, she washed and dried her hands, turned and came toward me, over to the door where I was still hanging on for dear life.

"Now, tell me," she started, very slow, very deliberate, "why did you walk all the way home to go to the bathroom?"

I could see that I was in for it.

"Is it that you don't like school?" She put her hands on my shoulders, bent down, tried to make me look her in the eye. My eyes clung to the doorknob as fiercely as my hands.

She shook me. "What's the matter with you?" Her fingers dug into my shoulders. "Well, all right," she straightened up, "you can just stand there . . . until you decide to answer me." Turning away, she went back to the pie crust, began rolling it out . . . .

And I knew it was true. That I would go on standing there. And that there would be no way out. Because I had come home to the bathroom for the same reason I was standing there like that — I could not bring out the words it took.

Finally, what I couldn't find the words for, Nature managed on its own. Standing there, I wet my pants.

"Tongue-tied, that's what the trouble is," Mother declared a few days later. "Open your mouth, Betty Jane." She looked in. "Lift your tongue." I lifted it. "Yes! That's what it is; your tongue's tied too far down."

Having decided there was nothing wrong that a surgeon's scissors couldn't "cut away," Mother took me to Dr. Martin. In among all the smiles and jokes he aimed her way, he took time out to look inside my mouth. "Yes, a simple thing, to snip that." He then returned his attention to Mother.

"You're not going to cut on her — I won't stand for it!" Nanna said, plopping her dishrag into the sudsy water, splashing bubbles up into the air under the kitchen light.

"She's *my* child!" Mother retorted.

"I wouldn't care if she was the nigger maid's child . . ."

". . . as though I don't have sense enough to rear my own child . . . ."

"You can have sense and still be wrong."

"If I can't be treated like a grown woman around here, I'll move out."

In our house, all arguments came down to this. And ended with my grandmother's trump card: "Just where do you think you can go?"

The appointment with Dr. Martin was cancelled. And soon afterward the speech lessons started again. In Mother's bedroom. This room.

At the age of seven, I was judged ready for another try at school.

As soon as I learned to read, I was expected to practice my speech lessons by myself, every day, for thirty minutes.

Since Mother died, sixteen months ago, I have practiced a full hour each day. A last attempt to find favor in her eyes.

5:45. Tired of Burke, I turn to *Antony and Cleopatra,* picture myself as Claudette Colbert, and begin: "Give me my robe, put on my crown; I have immortal longings in me."

6:00. I close the book, unplug the fan, and sit down on the bed, my mock tears turning to real ones. The silliness of it all, I think, of trying to please someone who, to hear Reverend Jenkins tell it, is beyond caring.

"Betty Jane!" The peremptory voice of Nanna, from the kitchen. "Supper's ready."

At the kitchen table I sit down to a tall glass of milk with sugar and chopped apple and yesterday's crumbled-up corn bread all stirred into it and with an iced-tea spoon sticking out of it. Since Mother died, Nanna hasn't bothered with cooking. Or with keeping house: all the rooms, except the kitchen and her bedroom and mine, are closed off — unaired, uncleaned, and, in winter, unheated.

Back in my bedroom I return the fan to the vanity and sit down to get ready for the party at Gary Stewart's house — wiping the perspiration from my face, patting it with Mother's powder, watching the shiny beads seep through the powder, collect into rivulets. Last, recalling Mother's exasperated, "For Heaven's sake! Read the paper and *find* something to say!" I go to the kitchen for the *Dixter Banner*.

Poor Mother. Never giving up on me. Not even at the last when she knew (but I didn't) that she couldn't live — coming up with the idea of sing-along parties where I wouldn't have to talk. Just last summer. The summer when the parties, for the first time, included boys.

I still remember how it was, sitting in the side yard on Nanna's quilts — the boys on one and the girls on the other — the smell of the freshly mowed grass mixing with the acrid smell of the burned orange peels in the incinerator, and the dark bulk of the First Baptist Church across the alley, its big dome reaching up into the light of the moon. And the lightning bugs, flicking on and off — not in time with the singing, but "in syncopation," Gary said. (Gary had had music lessons.)

Our favorite songs were "The Last Round-Up" and "Shuffle Off to Buffalo." At one of the parties, just after we rolled out the last notes of "How Dry I Am," we heard another song — coming to us, it seemed, from the great dome itself: "Throw out the lifeline, thro-o-w out the lifeline, someone is sinking today." Prayer meeting. Out in Reverend Jenkins's yard. Because of the heat indoors. We listened, imagined them sitting in their folding chairs, probably hearing us as we heard them. Sniggering, conspiring, we waited. As soon as they finished the last verse, we picked up with "Who's Afraid of the Big Bad Wolf?" They responded with "Onward, Christian soldiers, marching as to war." We came back with "Marching Along Together."

"A counterpoint," Mother later said to me, "between puberty and prayer."

"What's puberty?" I asked.

Now, at our parties, we dance. Sort of, because no one knows how. But at least I don't have to talk.

The party tonight is at Gary's house. All this summer he has been the one who walks me to the parties and home again. By the time cold weather comes, he'll be old enough to drive me in the car, and I'll be old enough to have real dates. Not just party dates.

What Gary and I have in common is words. With me, it's finding some; with him, it's finding new ones. At the last party, his new one was *emulate.* This does not make him popular with the other boys.

As Gary and I turn onto the front walk to his porch,

Mr. Stewart is pumping away with a Flit gun. "I could kill the damned things easier with my bare hands," he calls, evidently to Mrs. Stewart, inside, for we hear, "George!"

"Can't we turn the damned light off?" he calls.

"And leave the young people in the dark?" she appears at the door.

"We'll be sitting by the window, for God's sake."

The parents always sit by the window onto the porch, I have noticed. Mrs. Stewart, seeing us, opens the screen door and comes out. She is dressed in a blue and white voile. I am wearing a navy blue rayon crepe, with purple perspiration stains.

"You can help us set up the card table, out here on the porch," she greets us.

Cards? Our faces fall.

"It's too hot for dancing," she explains, "so I bought a new game. Monopoly."

Mr. Stewart laughs. "Does it give a boy an excuse to keep his arm around a girl?"

Mrs. Stewart gives him a hard look and goes inside.

I pretend a sudden interest in the potted geraniums on the porch railing. (Apart from dancing, Gary has never even put an arm around me.)

Gary seems embarrassed, too. "Want to meet my

grandmother?" he suggests.

"Oh, yes," I reply, glad of a new subject. "I've heard about her from Nanna." ("Poor soul, stuck off in the hottest room of the house. Upstairs, too, and her not able to manage stairs.")

As we reach the upstairs hall, I can see her profile against the light from the street lamp at the corner. At the door to her room, as Gary reaches for the light switch, I hold out my hand to stop him — she's surely sitting there ungirdled, I think, trying to get cool, the way Nanna does. Too late. The light comes on.

And there she's sitting — fully dressed. Like she was going somewhere. Looking nothing at all like any of the other old ladies in Dixter — all of *them* are stout, with that country directness that comes from years of wringing chickens' necks. She looks too frail, too genteel for the chicken yard.

"Grannybell, may I present Betty Jane Bledsoe?" Gary is saying, in that formal way of his that the other boys make fun of. "We're dancing tonight, Grannybell, to the Hit Parade."

"I'm sorry, dear?" she says. Perhaps she's hard of hearing.

"Top tunes. Radio," he explains.

142

"Oh, yes," she smiles, a pleasant, almost placid smile. Not at all like Nanna's smiles, which — like Marie Dressler's — smack of evil.

"Do you do the schottische?" she asks.

"Not in public," he grins.

"How this fellow teases me," she smiles. A small pause — then, "No one else bothers." Turning back to Gary, she asks, "What do you young men and women dance today?"

"The Carioca," I answer.

Gary looks at me as though I were speaking Icelandic.

"Well, in the dancing academies, anyway," I add, as though Dixter knew a dancing academy from a hay barn.

Gary has a wary look.

"Dolores Del Rio danced it in *Flying Down to Rio,*" I go on. The truth is, I read it in the *Banner,* looking for something to talk about.

Gary, who hasn't even mastered the fox-trot, changes the subject. "I'll bet in your day you had plenty of beaus, Grannybell."

"Allowed to come calling, only one — besides your grandfather." Getting up, crossing the narrow space between her chair and the chiffonier, she says, "I've been sorting my things . . . ."

"What things?" I wonder, looking around the empty, airless room. A chair. A chiffonier. A night table. A bed. Like a dentist's recovery room. I think of Nanna, charging through our big house and around our big yard, planting her vegetables and her flowers, tending her chickens. I think of the spacious and gracious rooms here in the Stewarts' house, of the master suite across the hall with its own sitting room and dressing room and bath.

"Railroad pictures," she explains, opening an old Whitman's sampler box she has pulled from a drawer. "A photographer would travel with the train, and people would go to the station and wait, to have their pictures made."

She picks out a picture, hands it to us. A brownish picture of a pop-eyed young man with a fine, delicate nose and mouth. "He's the one," she said, "the only other one. The only other man who ever kissed me, too." She stands very quiet. We also stand very quiet. "So sweet, his kisses were."

I sneak a look from the picture to her; she's smiling. I realize that for once I needn't be embarrassed for having nothing to say: she wasn't making conversation; she was just remembering — out loud.

The stillness continues.

144

"Well . . ." Gary announces, louder than necessary, turning me toward the door, "I think I hear the others." And out he pushes me, into the hall.

Going across the hall and down the stairs, I'm thinking about what Gary's father said and what his grandmother said. And thinking that everyone seems to know something I don't know but that they think I know. Or that I *will* know before long. And I'm hoping they're right, that maybe I will . . . around the turning of the landing, or the doorway to the entrance hall, around the corner of some evening, just like this one, I will know, and I, too, will have something to write down in a book and remember, the way Mother did.

As we step out onto the porch, the radio on the window sill declares that Number Eight this week is "Soon." Gary puts an arm around me and pulls me into the song; he smells of after-shave lotion. The music pours, thick and slow; we dance, lightly swaying. Beneath the music I hear the sound of the dancers' feet, shuffling, on the wooden porch, of the green bugs, buzzing, caught in the spell of the light falling through the window, falling from the lamp where the Stewarts sit reading. The dancers, too, move into the circle of light, across it, then fade again, into the dimness beyond. Now

Gary and I dance into the circle, hang there, suspended, by the words of the song. "Soon . . . maybe not tomorrow, but soon . . . ."

Back home, lying on my army cot in the side yard where we had the singing parties (where now, because of the heat, Nanna snoring beside me, we sleep), lying here smelling the greenness, looking at the dome of the First Baptist Church and the moon and the lightning bugs, I am filled with such a gladness as I've not felt since those nights of the singing. And the lightning bugs, I think, are winking at the moon about this gladness in the summer air.

"Wouldn't you just know?" It's Nanna, the next morning, all but wailing, coming down the hall from the library.

One of her gloom-and-doom announcements, probably. I'm in the bathroom, applying a paste of oatmeal and raw egg to my face — the *Woman's Home Companion* says it will keep the skin from sagging.

"I can't bear it, Lord," she stops at the door of the bathroom. "Well?" she asks. "Don't you want to know what it is I can't bear?"

"What?" I ask, turning my porridgey face toward her. She ignores it.

"It's Tom. He's coming to live with us."

("Who's Tom?" I wonder.) But she's off, heading through the pantry, holding an envelope in one hand, tapping it against the other.

"It's not fair," she declares, disappearing into the breakfast room.

I put the last bit of paste on my face, and she's back. "Went off and left me, you know, and me only a slip of a girl!"

I can think of nothing to say. Besides, my mask is hardening.

As she begins to realize I don't know who she's talking about, she says, "My brother. My big strapping grown brother. Just took the mule and rode off. Left me to fend for myself." Off she stomps, down the hall to the library, tapping that envelope. "Have mercy, Lord. Have mercy!"

At lunch I have to listen to the whole story — how after her parents died ("'the fever' they called it") out on the farm they sharecropped down in Texas, this practically grown brother "just upped and left." She was fourteen. (I am struck by the novel thought of my grandmother ever having been fourteen.) The preacher in the nearby town placed her in a home as a domestic.

Sixty-three years ago. In these years, her brother kept in touch just enough to borrow money.

She gets up from the table and walks to the door out onto the back porch, stands there looking out through the mulberry trees. "It's not fair," she says quietly, all the fight gone out of her. "Me, ending my days changing *his* sheets and washing *his* underwear . . . it's just not fair."

"Ain't much meat on her, is they," Uncle Tom says to Nanna upon meeting me. He's sitting in Nanna's rocker in her bedroom. She's in the closet taking down her dresses, tossing them across to the bed.

"Ella, I shore hate you have to move out," he says.

"How'd we manage if you fell, coming down the stairs to the bathroom?" (Our one bathroom is downstairs.)

"Let me unpack for you," I say, thinking it will be better than trying to find words to talk to him. Reaching down into his suitcase, I come up with what appears to be a gigantic dish towel, with armholes and legholes . . . .

"B.V.D.'s," Nanna says, seeing my bewilderment. "*Underwear,*" she explains.

Three stained and torn handkerchiefs, a pair of long underwear, three collarless shirts, one collar, a sweater, pajamas, a pair of trousers . . . .

"You been to Oklahoma before?" I ask, trying to start a conversation.

"Mmmm?" He looks at me, a vacuous grin on his face. "A smart time back. Down on the Red River."

While I put his things in the drawers Nanna has just emptied, I study him. Nearly all hands and head, on a frail frame. Great, long hands, hanging, inert. And a long head, hanging, just as inert.

At the bottom of the suitcase lie a leather razor strap, a folding razor, and a cigar box. In the box, denture polish, a comb, a broken pencil. Beside the suitcase, a shoebox. "My papers," he says, reaching out one of those huge hands.

"Where are the rest of your things?" I ask, looking around the room and out toward the hall.

"That'll do, Betty Jane," Nanna speaks up, sharp, cutting me off.

"What happened to Grannybell's belongings," I ask Gary, "when she moved in with you?" We are walking to a party at Mary Jo Keene's house.

"Sold them. Threw them away. Why?"

"Nothing."

"You should've seen him when he got out of the car! That old mulehead of his just a-beaming." Nanna has just deposited Uncle Tom at the corner of Main and Seventh, with money in his pocket for tobacco. He has been with us a week now. "Standing there with those other old geezers, chewin' and spittin'."

She's happy for him, I realize, surprised. I can't recall her being happy about Mother's friends — not even once.

That evening, the three of us sitting on the front porch hoping for a breeze, I listen to Uncle Tom, watch him, ask myself how this slack-jawed old man sitting there all sprawled out and hunched over, his head hanging out in front of him, could be Nanna's brother — and her so brisk, so straight (put herself into shoulder braces at forty to get rid of her seamstress's hump).

"Them candles is might purty, Ella," he says. It takes me a minute or so to realize he's talking about her cannas, out in the south flower bed.

150

And where did he get his country way of talking? *Him* — the one who got to go to high school, while Nanna had to go to work as a hired girl.

I begin to appreciate Nanna — a little.

"A heap purtier than them across the street," he's saying.

(The house across the street belongs to the Turners: he's the president of the Douglas County Oil Well Casing Company, south of town.)

"It sure gets to her, too," Nanna says. "Always asking me, she is, 'What makes yours prettier than mine?'" Getting one of her evil smiles on her face, Nanna says, "Wouldn't she just get a look on those rouged-up wrinkles of hers if I said to her, 'It's the chicken shit that does it!'"

Uncle Tom gives out a cackle, and I'm suddenly wondering what's got into Nanna . . . using dirty words.

"I made it across the tracks, all right," she says, "but I brought my chickens with me."

They both laugh. They are having a fine time.

"Sometimes I wish I'd brought the cow, too."

I'm remembering those stories I've always hated listening to — how it was her butter-and-egg money that bought the set of encyclopedia, how they never had an indoor bathroom because they were saving for the two girls to go to college . . . .

From the First Baptist Church comes the sound of singing. Prayer meeting tonight. Warming up on "Sweet Hour of Prayer."

"That's plumb purty," says Uncle Tom, beginning to rock in time with the music.

"You ever get yourself baptized, Tom?"

"Ain't one fer that," he says. For someone so indifferent, I think, he's sure engrossed, rocking away to the music. "Them hymns allus puts me in mind of Edna Prichard."

"I'd forgot all about Edna . . ." she says, picking up the beat in her rocking.

"Remember them camp meetings?" he asks.

"Land, yes. Clear over in Tyler County."

"Hitchin' the mule to the wagon . . ." he says.

They're rocking, almost in unison, slow and steady.

"Packin' up the quilts."

"Fryin' up the chicken."

"Back behind the wagon . . ." he says.

"Where you sneaked off with Edna."

"Kissed her, I did, while they was singin' 'Bringin' in the Sheaves.'"

"I don't know what's going to become of us," Nanna's saying, looking out at the dead grass and the dying cannas.

She's at it again, I think, old Jeremiah herself.

"All this heat. And no rain. I've never seen the likes of it . . . ."

Everyone now is beginning to sound like Nanna, talking like it's the end of the world. And it might as well be, for me and Gary and Mary Jo and the others, what with all the parents saying that with the thermometer standing at 109 degrees at nine o'clock, porch parties are out of the question. And none of us old enough to drive, so the only thing we can do is walk to the Palace for the seven-thirty movie, with the sun still way up in the sky. Walking home, it's no better, with the tire store and the filling station and the furniture store all lighted up like day.

Mostly, Gary and I sit on the porch with the Stewarts or with Nanna. The lightning bugs are gone. The air has a brown, dusty smell. And there we are, Nanna saying What's-to-become-of-us? and me thinking I'll grow old and never be kissed, that's what. (I've started the oatmeal and egg packs, again.)

The Stewarts are sending Gary to boarding school in

September.

Uncle Tom no longer joins us on the porch. He's fading as fast as the cannas. He lies in Nanna's bed, propped up on nearly every pillow in the house, his mouth open, his eyes staring out the window toward the scorched garden.

For the most part, I have to admit that Nanna's been more than fair to Uncle Tom. Given him better than he earned.

Except once.

One night, while Nanna and I were eating our supper, he must have decided he could make it to the bathroom on his own. Got as far as the hall. But too late. So, then he tried to clean it up and, weak as he is, fell right into it.

That's when we heard him, from out in the kitchen.

Just by itself, it was enough to turn my stomach. But that wasn't the worst of it. The worst was Nanna, screaming at him about how it's only right he had a head as long as a mule's and asking him over and over *why didn't he call her* — and all the time him cowering there against the wall, making little whimpering objections, like a dog being beaten by his master, and me standing there ashamed of her and sorry for him and deep inside cowering just like he was, remembering how once I couldn't find the words to ask to go to the bathroom — or to explain it afterward to Mother.

When we finally got him and the hallway washed up, Nanna fired one last volley — this one for me. "Mark my words — that daddy of yours'll show up some day — on *your* doorstep!"

No one can say Nanna hasn't done her best to make Uncle Tom comfortable. At the foot of his bed she has rigged up an old clothes-drying rack covered with wet towels, with a big fan blowing through them toward Uncle Tom. We take turns keeping the towels wet.

But it's useless. His sheets are always soaked with perspiration, even though we change them three times a day. Ethel has been coming in every day to wash them, in the big copper kettle in the basement. So, I know he's going to die. (The only times Nanna has Ethel come to help us is when somebody is dying.)

Though Nanna lets me help with changing the sheets and dipping the towels, she insists on doing the bed-pan work herself, and on bathing him, and changing his pajamas. "Think how embarrassed he'd be, having you do it." She's looking older every day. In spite of myself,

I'm beginning to feel sorry for her.

I've given up doing the speech practice. I'm not sure why. It seems like everybody's just waiting for the end — of one thing or another. The gloomy ones, for the end of the world; the hopeful, for a rain; Uncle Tom, for an end to his days; Nanna and I, waiting with him; and me — I'm waiting for Gary; and Gary — I don't know whether he's waiting or just needs a little gumption.

As talking to Uncle Tom is harder than ever these days, I'm grateful this morning when he says, "Could 'ee fetch me my papers?"

The shoebox . . . middle drawer . . . I hand it to him.

He fumbles through it, frowns, pours the entire contents out on the bed, paws around through the papers, gets a little frantic . . . .

"Can I help?" I ask.

Out of breath, he lays his head back on his stack of pillows. "The tax receipt."

"You want me to look for it?"

He nods.

Every single piece of paper has been folded and refolded, is yellow and brittle with age. Carefully unfolding each one, I find recipes for cures for a cold, old I.O.U.'s . . . .

Nanna comes in. "What is it, Tom?"

"The Mexico property. The tax receipt."

"You haven't paid the taxes?" Leave it to Nanna, to guess, right off.

He isn't sure, he says, doesn't want it sold for delinquent taxes. "It'll be good for Betty Jane to have."

"All right, Tom, I'll see to the taxes, don't you worry."

"Might be oil under it, some day."

"That's right, Tom," she says indulgently, as she leaves the room.

As I try to put together some words to say thanks, he says, "I'd jes be obliged if you'd read me from that there book." He points toward the dresser, toward a small, red, imitation-leather book marked *Accounts*.

Opening it, I begin: "1889. Due Tom Winters, for picking cotton, $11.40." "Is this what you mean?" I ask, thinking it must be the wrong book. But seeing him lying there, his eyes closed, as though I were reading poetry, I go on: "Due Tom Winters, hire hand for Jess Miller, $15.80. Due Tom Winters, hire hand for Tab Wheeler, $27.50."

"Old Tab — he took to drink," he says.

"Expenses: board — $1.00, shirt — .30, hoe — .60, sugar — $2.00, tobacco — .50, snuff — .30." One, just like another, I read off the next eight years of his life, while he listens, blissful.

Then I come to a page that's different from the others. Not all filled with scrawls. This one has nothing on it but one note — centered, neat, like the note in Mother's textbook:

Tom G. Winters
Moved awn . . . November 19, 1907

"Where did you go, Uncle Tom?" He's lying there, looking like I'd laid a blessing on him.

"Mexico."

I wait, but decide that's all he has to say on the subject. Then, just as I'm about to turn the page, he says, "Saw the mountains. Never figgered I'd see nothin' like that . . . ." He opens his eyes, looks across the wet towels at the blank wall. "Put me in mind of a preacher, once, talkin' 'bout a man who seen Jesus, sayin' how he could die happy, now . . . ."

"'Now lettest thou thy servant depart in peace,'" I hear myself saying.

"Somethin' like that, it was." He closes his eyes, and I'm about to turn back to the book when he says, "It allus bothered me — my folks goin' to their graves and never seein' what I seen."

"Shall I go on?" I ask. He nods.

"1901 — cultivated twenty-six acres; 1910 — cultivated fifty acres; 1911 — cultivated eighty-five acres."
Then a two-page listing of twenty-eight varieties of fruit
trees he had planted — all, no doubt, with great hope
that in that sandy desert soil they would somehow thrive
and bear.

"Jes be sure to keep them taxes paid — may be oil
under that there land."

"Goat land," Nanna says as we're washing up the
dishes that night. "But even an old cur dog likes to leave
tracks."

"But it's sweet of him to . . ." I persist.

"It makes him feel good. Even if it *is* just one more
thing to pay taxes on." She laughs. "Perked him up
almost as much as those prayer meetings — with him
lying there listening so hard you'd think he'd got himself
saved, and all the time him thinking about kissing Edna
Prichard." She laughs again. "Well, it's high time those
meetings brought somebody some good!"

Her face turns somber (she's like that — she can turn

on you in mid-sentence). "I doubt he'll make it 'till next week's meeting."

Although she'd told me about the spell he had this afternoon when I was out and about the doctor coming, I'd paid no special attention. The truth is, I was thinking about seeing Gary tonight, wishing *we* had a camp meeting to go to, or that Gary had a little imagination.

"You liked those camp meetings, too, didn't you?" I ask.

"More than anything else from back then, I remember those."

"Why?" I ask. After all, she would have been too young for sneaking off behind a wagon.

"Why, the singing!" she says.

"The *singing?*" I repeat.

"You bet. The only music we ever knew, besides the church piano — when we could get to a church."

At first, I'm dubious. Then I remember the parties here, out in the yard, the mowed grass and the acrid oranges in the incinerator and the big dome and the moon.

"Course, it wasn't any of that puling, draggy singing they do over there today. Pious singing, I call it. No, sir, not ours. Nobody held back, no matter how raspy-throated they were. We may have got everything else wrong, but we got that rhythm right. And when we'd get going good, the preacher would call out, 'Let 'em hear it over in Bowie,' and we'd let go a little louder." Her face is all lit up, with the memory. "Bowie was clear over the ridge," she smiles.

"Why don't you ever sing, now?"

"I'll bet I could still sing every word from every one of those songs," she declares. "There's some things a person doesn't forget."

She starts in: "I love to tell the st-o-o-ry, of Jee-sus a-a-nd his love . . ." Her voice is hollow and wavery, but no one can say it's weak or timorous.

As she gets the feel of it, finds the rhythm, I join in: "T'will be my theme in Glory, To tell the old, old story . . ." And there we stand, the two of us, her with a dish rag and cream-dipper in her hands, me with a towel and a serving platter, singing full voice, all throttles out — me missing the high notes, her, the low.

Finishing the last verse, we're so pleased with ourselves we start in again, this time, "Stand up, stand up for Jesus," her beating the time, march-like, on the wooden drainboard, me hoisting a plate over my head like a banner.

161

At the end of it, both of us are laughing and out of breath. It is, so far as I can recall, the first time we have laughed together since Mother died.

"Tell you what," she gives me a knowing grin, "let's give him a treat."

"What?" I ask, not understanding.

"The one they were singing when he kissed Edna Prichard."

And so we sing. "Bringing in the Sheaves." Loud and strong, making sure he can hear us in there, propped up in front of the fan and the towels.

When it's over, our grinning seems to have gone out of us. We just stand there, quiet. Maybe sad. The light that had filled her face drains away; she takes a long deep breath and says, "I wonder. What was the use of it?"

"Of the singing?" I ask.

"Of all the work and all the scrimping and the doing-without. And all your mother's studying and your aunt's . . . and both of them dead, so young. I just wonder. What was the use?"

I remember asking myself the same question, about me and my practicing.

Nanna's hands are just lying there in the dishwater, like she'd forgotten where she left them, and she's looking out the window, through the wilted crepe myrtle. "From my folks to my girls — laying them all in the ground. Was that all I was put here for?"

I don't know what to say.

In another of her abrupt switch-abouts, she turns from the window, her face stern, and looks me straight in the eye. "Unless it's *you*," she says.

Me again. To lay it all on *me*. All the wasted learning — and the sacrifice. All at my feet. A tongue-tied girl who can't even see her way past her first kiss.

It's not fair, I think.

Then I remember. That's exactly what *she* said, the day the letter came from Uncle Tom.

And I remember the encyclopedia bought with the butter-and-egg money . . .

And the indoor bathroom traded for the college degree . . .

And the hours Mother spent spooning words into my mouth . . .

I go into my bedroom, unplug the small, buzzing fan on the vanity, move it to the middle of the floor, and, reaching under the bed, plug it in. Then, taking four volumes of the *Encyclopedia Americana*, I lie down and . . .

THE VOICE IN THE
IN THE
WHIRLWIND

T WAS IN HIS PARENTS' storm cellar that Homer Henson lost his virginity to Lavinia Wright — but that's another story. I mention it here only to show that, growing up in Dixter, we spent a lot of time in storm cellars. Geography is fate. For Dixter, besides being in the Dust Bowl and the Bible Belt, is smack on the centerline of Tornado Alley.

Newcomers to Tornado Alley — like the geologists and engineers who moved here from back East during the oil boom of the Twenties — would say you'd never catch *them* down in one of those ready-made graves, would say even a nitwit ought to know enough not to pile all the dirt back on top of the hole he dug it from, with nothing but a few rotting timbers to hold it up.

But people who lived through the Dixter Tornado of '98, when the whole town blew off the map, would just

167

smile and say, "I don't recall as anyone died in his storm cellar." That summer of '98 was when my grandmother, a young bride, learned to pay attention to the voice in the whirlwind.

The way she told the story, she was canning her first crop of green beans, and she wouldn't have left them, storm or no, if it hadn't been for Mrs. Richardson calling out to her the way she did. The Richardsons, who lived down the draw where Hog Wallow Creek crossed the low-water bridge, were city-folk. And poor to boot. They'd not seen fit to dig a storm cellar — or even to plant a vegetable garden.

"But she found our storm cellar quick enough all right, that afternoon, when the sky got black and the wind came up. I was in my kitchen, sterilizing my jars — keeping an ear on the wind, you can be sure — but as I had my fire going good, I wasn't planning to waste it.

"Well, I heard this yelling, and someone calling my name, so I went over to the window — and the sight I saw — it made me think my green beans had best wait. There was that puny little woman, hanging onto the cellar door for dear life, and the wind holding onto both of them and banging them up and down like it was shaking a rug."

Nanna dried her hands and ran out, and between the

two of them, they managed to get down into the cellar before the tornado itself hit down.

Coming out after the storm, looking up the draw, Nanna saw the Richardsons' house, with not so much as a shingle blown loose, and she was miffed with herself — leaving her green beans like that. Then she turned around and saw — over where her own house had been — nothing. Just the foundation, clean as the day it was laid. Looking on down the pasture, she found the rest of the house, a little tipsy and disarranged but still standing, giving out occasional hiccoughs as, piece by piece, the broken glass fell from its windows.

So it was only to be expected that when my grandparents, some years later, built their big new house on the fancier side of town (no cow lots, no outhouses), it would have the biggest basement in Dixter — big enough for everyone on the block, dogs and all.

What my grandparents couldn't foresee was that the First Baptist Church, also moving to the fancy side of town, would be built right aross the alley — a great, huge, hulking thing with a fake marble front copied after the pagan Parthenon and a high dome copied after the papist St. Peters. From then on, everyone on the block (including my grandparents) took to going to Mrs. Mil-

169

ler's storm cellar: no one wanted to end up in our basement buried under the transplanted bulk of the First
Baptist Church.

At the storm vigil I remember best (the summer before
my sophomore year in high school), seven of us plus a dog
crowded into her cellar — besides Mrs. Miller and
Nanna and me, there was Mrs. Sims, Reverend Jenkins
(the Baptist preacher), a new neighbor (Mrs. Kyle),
Sylvie Winters, and Sylvie's dog, Taddy.

Everyone along South Tenth Street knew Sylvie and
Taddy, because six days a week, on unspecified errands of
great urgency and great haste, they would pass our houses
on the way to town and back; she, muttering and frowning and arguing with unseen adversaries; he, lordly and
complacent and, often as not, looking out from the
cradle of her arms. For though to our eyes Taddy was a
common enough mutt — short legs, short hair (black
and white) — to Sylvie he was as precious as an only-
and-late-life child, and she would not risk his getting
"frozed feet" or "heat-strucked."

All Dixter laughed about "that poor child and her
dog," her a slight thing weighing hardly a hundred

pounds, lugging that beast who weighed a good thirty, her with dull, uncared-for hair, him with a shining, well-brushed coat.

"That poor child" was getting on toward forty years of age.

While Sylvie never spoke to anyone, her sister Nell spoke to everyone. At length. And while Sylvie was always beset with concern, Nell was always full of smiles. She was simple-minded.

Sylvie, though, was downright crazy. Both were epileptic. Their parents dead, they still lived in the four-room frame house where they'd grown up. Giving no one any trouble, no one troubling them. Nor helping. It was assumed that Nell's "business" — selling embroidered pillow cases, crocheted doilies, and antimacassars from door to door, winter and summer — brought in enough money for their needs. Besides, none of us wanted to know differently.

Nell and Sylvie had become one of our fondest local legends, one that made us feel good about ourselves — for letting them live in their house, unbothered.

But at the time of the storm, they had become "that crazy pair." Sylvie had got herself raped. A gang of boys — from Tallisaw, obviously. (In our world view everything noxious came from Tallisaw). Sylvie didn't know there was a name for what happened to her, but she was able to tell Nell about it when she came home, and Nell went next door and told their neighbor, and the neighbor called a doctor.

The town tried to show sympathy; that is, people would stop Nell on her rounds and ask about Sylvie — even though experience had long since taught them that once Nell opened her mouth, she never knew when to shut it.

Before long they began to notice her stories always seemed to lead to, "Throws up every morning, she does, just like Mother did, afore she was took." Her mother had died of an obstructing tumor. The way the town figured, this was no tumor.

Overnight, Sylvie became "a disgrace to Dixter." "Us so good to 'em — and what's our thanks? Another idjit, like as not." Some, remembering the violence of its conception, said, "a crazy mother and a criminal father — we'll see the day it might murder us in our beds."

Such thoughts, however, paled in the light of the more troubling question — right in its head or not, who was to take care of it?

Spectres of Christian duty danced before the towns-peoples' eyes. A committee of church ladies spoke with Reverend Jenkins. "The Lord will provide," he told them.

"But not out of church money, you can just bet," Nanna prophesied, on hearing about it.

"It ought to be got rid of," declared no less a luminary than Mrs. Greenwood, president of the Ladies Missionary Society. Encouraged by her audacity, others dared to agree — though they left it to her to test Reverend Jenkins's reaction, using as their excuse, "The way things come out of *her* mouth, they sound so proper."

"Fair flustered him, it did," Mrs. Sims reported to Nanna, third-hand from Mrs. Caulfield, out on our front porch, with me listening at the library window.

After that, for the longest time, I could hear nothing but the sound of their cane rockers; then Nanna, in a musing voice, said, "Remember old Reverend Bewley?"

"Land, yes, a body couldn't forget that good soul."

"Well, Reverend Bewley always said," the rocking stopped, "we shouldn't push our dirty work off onto the

Lord. Said the Lord's work, on this earth, was *our* work."
The rocking resumed; there was no other sound.

That's pretty much how matters stood, the day of the
tornado. When the hail became the size of hens' eggs and
the wind began whipping the tree branches like handsful
of posies, Nanna and I were already on our way to Mrs.
Martin's storm cellar. Across the street we saw Mrs.
Sims, her fat arms cushioning her head from the hail-
stones, hurrying her three-hundred-pound heft through
her side-gate. Then we saw Sylvie, her print dress
soaked, clinging to her body like a wrinkled, tattooed
skin, the hail bouncing from her unprotected head,
while Taddy, secure and snug, lay in her sheltering arms.

We could see Mrs. Sims's mouth working, like she was
calling out to Sylvie, but with the wind roaring so, we
couldn't hear her; and if Sylvie heard, she gave no sign,
just hunched herself into the wind and the rain. Mrs.
Sims, heaving her way to the sidewalk, wasting no time
on persuasion, wrapped her fat arms around Sylvie and
the dog and — looking like she was dragging a load of wet
wash — hustled them along with her.

As Nanna and I reached Mrs. Miller's yard, Mrs. Sims

174

was trying to keep her hold on Sylvie and the dog with one arm, reaching down with the other for the door — and losing her hold on all three. Sylvie — it was obvious — was not going down into that hole; Mrs. Sims — it was just as obvious — was not going to leave her out in the storm; so there, beside that mound of earth, with the lightning flashing in the daytime-darkness of the sky, with their hair streaming water and their eyes skewed up against the hail, they were battling it out, like a soul and the Devil.

Suddenly the door lifted up — sucked up by the wind, I thought, until I saw the hands and then the arms following them up from below . . . like the arms of lost souls reaching up from hell-fire.

The arms, as it turned out, belonged to Mrs. Miller and Mrs. Kyle and Reverend Jenkins, who were giving the door a boost against the wind. Nanna and I, coming up, grabbed the door, and Mrs. Sims pushed Sylvie and the dog down the stairs.

Down inside, Mrs. Miller had lighted a candle — the cellars were never without candles and matches and candleholders, which in the case of Homer Henson and Lavinia Wright may have been romantic, but in ours was only sinister. Looking around at our faces, transformed

175

by the shadows wavering across them, I could understand the terror I saw in Sylvie's eyes: Mrs. Miller, wild-eyed, her wiry gray hair shooting out like Medusa's snakes; Mrs. Sims, resembling a Buddha someone had turned a hose on; poor featureless Mrs. Kyle — a bowl of punched-down dough ready for the second rising; and Reverend Jenkins — with his round bald head and bright, wide-open eyes and fat, shiny cheeks — a middle-aged cherub. Even Nanna, a handsome, older woman — if somewhat stout — might have been on her way to the heath to meet Macbeth. (Once more, as so many times before, I promised myself that when I grew up, I'd live out in the *real* world with *real* people — like Norma Shearer and Leslie Howard.)

After the niceties of greetings, after lining ourselves up facing each other on the six-inch-wide wooden benches that ran, parallel, the length of the cellar, we were at a loss how to arrange our knees and feet — and, not least, our eyes.

Reverend Jenkins studied the high, flimsy timbers of the ceiling; Nanna studied her hands, while I checked out the dirt floor — relieved to find no standing water and comparatively little mud ("three inches of water underfoot and three feet of soil overhead" was the way the Easterners described our storm cellars).

Then, last, I dared to look for the thin beam of light that would tell me the air vent was not clogged up — with a bird's nest or a wasps' nest. All of these bodies, in that earthen hole, on a hot summer day, dependent on what was little more than a big straw — if it had been left up to me, I'd have taken my chances out there in the wind and the lightning.

Besides there being so little of it, the air seemed to be coming to us secondhand — laden with Mrs. Miller's whiskey breath and with Mrs. Sims's special blend of sweat and talcum and baking soda (the talcum, to soak up her sweat; the baking soda, to soothe the gall between her fat thighs). Everywhere she went, she was enveloped in white clouds, like the moon on a hazy night.

As for now, she was getting right to work on the new neighbor, Mrs. Kyle. "You're from Jackson County, I'll jis' warrant."

"No, I . . ."

"I'd a'sworn you're from Jackson County — the way you hang out your wash."

Mrs. Kyle had that should-I-laugh look that people get

when they think they've missed a joke.

"Comes from reachin' it from one persimmon to t'other — a leg on this 'un, an arm on that 'un — stretch a pair of longhandles nigh to ten feet, they kin. Give 'em a clothesline an' it don't change 'em none."

What's got into her? I wondered. I'd heard she had a mean streak in her — some even said her family perked up, bright as anything, every time she came down sick. But I'd never seen it myself.

The truth was, Mrs. Sims knew full well — just like everyone else in town knew — that the Kyles had moved here from Tallisaw. Everyone knew because everyone was talking about it, how in Dixter she was putting on respectable airs — "her, as has been *what she was!*" Even my friends and I, with only scanty notions about anatomy and with vast misinformation about sex and having babies, knew that Mrs. Kyle was one of those women a girl could go to if she got in trouble. "Brews her own medicine," Mary Jo Keene said; "Uses an ice pick," Earlene Wade said. Our conjectures were as endless as our ignorance.

Not long after the Kyles had moved in across the street from us, Nanna had taken them some okra from her garden, and she and Mrs. Kyle had hit it off right away.

"Common as pig tracks, all right," Nanna told me, after returning home, "but salt of the earth."

Of all people — Nanna, who was never fooled by anyone, not even by the con man who peddled the worthless oil stock to half the town (including the president of the bank). Wouldn't some of them just love to see Nanna taken in?

I'd have to warn her.

But it wouldn't be easy. Because the closest she and I had ever come to such a subject was the time she told me what I should do if a boy tried to put his arm around me. ("Slap him.")

She was working at the kitchen table, cutting up old house dresses to make aprons. (Nanna did all her cutting in the late afternoon, when the sun was coming through the west windows onto the kitchen table, which served as her cutting board.) After I got the words out, she just went right on — cutting away. Finally, when she had cut loose the section of pattern pinned to the center gore, she looked up at me with that wicked grin she had when she'd got the best of someone. "Yes," she said, "that's what I've heard, too."

"Then why do you . . . ?" I started to ask . . . but how does a girl go about instructing her grandmother in right

179

from wrong?

A few days later, coming into the kitchen after school and finding Nanna and Mrs. Kyle, their heads together, having a fine old time, I decided a sterner tack was in order. (I had my reputation to think of.)

So that night I brought it up again. She was sitting in the library, under the lamp with the beaded, fringed shade (the one she and Mother always said would be the first thing they'd get rid of if they got some money). With a skirt that had belonged to Mother in one hand and a razor in the other, she was pulling and cutting the seams, to make it over for me. Her eyes never leaving the seam, her mouth took on that tight, set look that had been known to put even Reverend Jenkins into retreat; now, with her false teeth removed for the night, it was more than enough to give me second thoughts.

"Think you know a lot about it, don't you?" She started to break off a thread with her teeth, realized she didn't have them. "Protected, like you've been," she cut it with the razor. "At your age, I'd been working out, two years — a hired girl."

I might have known. All issues, it seemed, came down to this: the story of her past. This time, at least, it turned out to be one I hadn't heard — about a hired girl who got pregnant and was kicked out, with no place to go. New story or old, I was certain the moral would be the same: how lucky I was, how grateful I should be, having a home, and her.

But she surprised me. "You think it's the likes of Mrs. Kyle that makes for bad girls?" Suddenly absorbed in her bifocals, I didn't answer — a strand of the blue crystal fringe of the lampshade, reflected in her glasses, was making her look for all the world as though she were crying sapphires. "Well, in my day, *that* kind had to drop them in the creek. Some married ones, too — the poor ones." Laying the razor down on the lamp table, letting the skirt fall in her lap, she seemed suddenly to have lost interest; she was absorbed in massaging the knuckles of two fingers of her right hand. They were enlarged, knobby, I noticed. But *when* had it happened? Surely, just recently . . . something inside me turned over with a thump . . . . Could Nanna be growing old? Could Nanna, the focus of all my angers and all my resentments, be deserting the field? To my great dismay, I was afraid. Surely, I thought, nothing could happen to *Nanna?*

That was when I realized, for the first time, that she was right: I was lucky to have her.

181

Picking up the skirt again, she asked in a low quiet voice, "What would you say if I told you I tried to get rid of your Little Auntie?"

I had visions of her trying to drown her, like those others, in the creek.

"Took castor oil. For three days." She reached for the razor. "Made me plenty sick, I can tell you." She slashed through the placket, severing the front panel from the back. "But I didn't lose her." Laying the razor down, she reached up under her glasses, wiped away a sapphire tear. "And didn't I remember all that — when the Lord took her from me, and her only twenty-five. I just knew he was punishing me."

Normally, Nanna wasn't one to talk about the Lord handing out punishments, said it was the wrong way to think about Him.

Pulling away the cut thread, she said, "Mrs. Kyle's what in my day we called a midwife. Out of style now. Called a practical nurse, instead. And other things we won't mention. Helped many a baby into this world, though. When the mothers didn't have money for a doctor. Didn't have husbands, either, as often as not."

"You mean it's all lies? About her?" I asked, hoping she'd say "Yes" and we could have done with it. But she said, "No. But if I'd known a Mrs. Kyle, I'd've gone to her, more than likely. Because we were poor, your grand-daddy and I, and I'd just had your mother, and your granddaddy had taken to drinking." She laid the skirt on the arm of the chair, put the razor on the table, got up, and switched off the lamp. "No, sir, you don't know a thing about it, you don't — what it's like . . . ."

And she walked out of the library, down the hall, and on back to her bedroom.

Left standing there in the semi-darkness, with only the light of the hallway falling through the library door, I was wrestling with new and terrible ideas — of Nanna getting old, of her dying, and, of the very clear pos-sibility that she wouldn't end up in Reverend Jenkins's Heaven.

"Tallisaw!" Mrs. Sims was still at it. "Don't usually git nuthin' but trouble from down their way . . . ."

Reverend Jenkins tried to pour oil on the troubled waters. "And a good choice you made, I must say. Dixter's got as God-fearing a group of people as you'll find anywhere."

Taddy, who up until now had been lying peaceably in

Sylvie's arms, submitting to her murmuring and croon-
ing, began to wriggle and to whimper — at which Sylvie
only clutched him tighter, all the while sneaking fearful
looks at each of us, as though convinced we had designs
on him. The closer she held him, the louder he whined
and the more he flopped about, until finally, with one
big twist and a lunge he popped free, like a cork out of a
bottle — only to find himself in a sprawl on a floorful of
feet. Panicked, stumbling and scrambling along, he
made his way across us to the stairs, up the stairs to the
door, which — with the wind outside gaining force —
was banging and shaking in its frame as though it too
were fighting to wrest itself free. There, with his front
feet on the top stair, he raised his head and began to howl
— in a mournful duet with the wind.

Sylvie, of course, was not far behind, stumbling across
us, cooing as she went, "It's all right, baby, it's all right,"
while Taddy only wailed louder. Again, Reverend
Jenkins took matters into his own hands; standing up and
stretching over, he grabbed the dog by the front legs and
handed him — his back legs threshing like an egg-beater
— across to Sylvie.

"Bless you, Reverend," pronounced Mrs. Sims.

With Taddy and Sylvie quiet, with Mrs. Sims having

let up on Mrs. Kyle, we had nothing to distract us from
the mounting din of the storm, from wondering, with
each rip and crash, whether it was a tree — or a house.
Our own house, even.

"Laws!" exclaimed Mrs. Sims, "don't I wish I knowed
where Mr. Sims is at!"

"And Mr. Kyle!" echoed Mrs. Kyle.

As on cue, we let out a sigh.

"I think we should pray," intoned Reverend Jenkins,
"for those abroad in the whirlwind."

Taddy, however, was not to be assuaged by prayer.
Once more, he popped out of Sylvie's arms, landing this
time on the back side of the benches. Freedom, we soon
learned, was not what he was looking for: sniffing along
until he came to the corner of one of the benches, he
paused, sniffed again — and again — then lifted his leg.

Right on past the leg of the bench it came, straight
onto Mrs. Miller's skirt, not entirely missing Reverend
Jenkins's pants. Then, not to show partiality, he sniffed
his way to the corner of the other bench, dropped a
different sort of present.

And us already about to gag for fresh air.

Mrs. Miller stared down at her skirt, like she was
figuring what to make of it, then her hand slid into the

185

pocket of her smock, coming out with a bottle of the medicine she was known to favor. This dose, I noticed, was about two inches.

"I'm goin' to throw up, fer sure," announced Mrs. Kyle.

"Take more'n that to unsettle *my* stomach!" boasted Mrs. Sims. "'S many diapers as I've changed, I could change a dirty 'un with one hand and eat a steak dinner with t'other."

"Leastways, we *could* move down," volunteered Mrs. Kyle, "so's the rest of you could move out of it."

While Mrs. Miller and Reverend Jenkins and I, at our end, were involved in the delicate business of repositioning ourselves, Sylvie and Mrs. Kyle and Mrs. Sims, on their end, seemed to be involved in some sort of commotion. "The derned dog," I was thinking; then there was some shoving, and then Nanna's voice, in one of her bossiest tones, barking at Mrs. Kyle, "Here! What's got into you!" And then I was thinking, "Better the dog than Nanna on one of her high horses!"

Turning around, I saw . . . what looked for all the world like Mrs. Kyle throwing a full tackle on Sylvie. And then Nanna, jumping to her feet, reaching for Mrs. Kyle, "Get hold of yourself!"

Now Mrs. Sims, too, was on her feet — and grabbing . . . for Sylvie? Or for Mrs. Kyle? I couldn't make it out, because, standing in that narrow space, they were like people waiting in line, fighting to get ahead of each other; besides, Mrs. Sims's heft was blocking not only my view, but the light of the candle, from down at our end.

But one thing I heard — quite clearly — over the sounds of the huffing and the scuffling: Mrs. Sims's voice, declaring matter-of-factly, "One o' her fits."

"A fit?" Nanna was asking; and then, "You're right." And before I knew it, she'd turned around and was herding me and Mrs. Miller and Reverend Jenkins back — straight into Taddy's mess. "Got to give them room," she explained.

"Git her 'round the shoulders," Mrs. Kyle ordered someone.

"Then you git her legs," Mrs. Sims replied.

While Mrs. Kyle and Mrs. Sims divided Sylvie up into arms and legs, while faces appeared and disappeared, while those grappling bodies grunted and snorted, and while Taddy wailed, I watched and listened with growing recognition: I'd known it all before, had it painted for me . . . how many times? By how many Baptist preachers? The damned, the lost souls, in the fiery lake.

How rank with specifics those descriptions had been — eyes bulging with fear, tongues hanging out with thirst, arms imploring, voices shrieking and moaning — and overall, the flickering light cast by fire.

And in contrast, how bland and nebulous their descriptions of Heaven — just a mooshy whiteness. Like mashed potatoes.

"Watch 'er head," Mrs. Sims wheezed.

"Ease 'er down now," Mrs. Kyle said.

"In this muck?"

"Cain't be dainty."

Poor Sylvie, I thought. Wrestled down into the lake of fire. As her face disappeared into the darkness beneath the benches, where even the shadows failed, her eyes looked as though they'd been granted a last, and supernatural, vision. Then there was no more to be seen of her but one thin white hand, reaching up, into the faint light, before it, too, sank into the dark.

Mrs. Kyle, bending over — her dress hiked up behind, revealing the knots she'd twisted into the tops of her stockings in place of garters, and above them, her fat dimply thighs — called out, "Got a fountain pen on ye, Reverend?"

Reaching into his pocket, he handed one across. Taking it with her free hand, she thrust it down into the darkness, withdrew her other hand, shaking it. "Quite a bite the girl's got!"

"Ain't the driest bed a body ever laid on," huffed Mrs. Sims, standing back a ways.

"Cain't balance her on them planks," replied Mrs. Kyle, pulling herself up. "Anyways, you saved her head, you did."

"Somethin' to be said fer my paddin'." Somewhere, in that darkness, it seemed that Mrs. Sims must have decided on a truce with Mrs. Kyle.

With Sylvie sleeping, peaceful as on a featherbed, with the rest of us arranging our legs around her as best we could, a loud crash across the cellar door reminded us of the world and the storm outside — the door, I felt sure, was going to disintegrate before our eyes.

"If that don't fair beat Job!" declared Mrs. Sims.

The cellar was suddenly darker.

I turned, looked for the thin beam of light: it was still there. But fainter.

"Just check that vent-pipe," Nanna whispered to Reverend Jenkins. Losing no time, he was standing on the bench, peering up. "Seems open — but like it was open onto twilight, instead of mid-afternoon."

189

We sat in silence, dismal with conjecture. Mrs. Miller reached in her smock, had another two-inch dose of her medicine.

Picking up the candle, Mrs. Kyle bent down for a look at Sylvie. "They'd best be diggin' us outa here purdy soon," she said.

"Something *else* wrong?" asked Nanna.

"Bleeding," Mrs. Kyle replied.

"Is the child injured?" inquired Reverend Jenkins. "Careful as you were?"

"Ain't that. More like you said, Reverend, the Lord is providing."

"Miscarrying?" asked Nanna.

"Mighty like," she answered.

"The Lord be praised!" exclaimed Reverend Jenkins.

"Amen!" whispered Nanna.

And then a chorus of "Amens." From everyone except Mrs. Miller.

Before we had time to start worrying again, we heard Mr. Sims, calling from outside, "You in there, Effie?"

From all of us, a chorus of "Yes!"

"Remember that elm, Effie? The one out by the alley?" Mr. Sims called.

"I don't care shoot 'bout no elm! Just git us outa here!"

190

Mrs. Sims yelled back, then turning to us with a look of disgust, said in a lowered voice, "Ain't that a man fer ye?"

"Well . . . I just mentioned it — because it's across the door here."

He left, to go for a saw.

The sound of his sawing . . . then the light streaming down on us through the opened door — it reminded me of that beam of light pouring down from Heaven on Jesus in the picture behind the baptismal pool (where Sammy Nell King came up out of the water with her red plaid dress showing loud as day through the soaked choir robe they'd put on her for her baptizing). And then the sound of the birds . . . it was better than Easter.

Stepping down a couple of steps, Mr. Sims lowered his head for a look at who was down here. "Whew!" and he stepped back up, got a gulp of air, made another try.

"Who's that?" he pointed to Sylvie, sleeping, there on the floor beneath us.

"Sylvie Winters. Done throwed a fit. And mebbe her baby 'long with it," explained Mrs. Sims.

"Yes . . . well," said Reverend Jenkins, turning toward Mr. Sims, "if you'll just give me a hand, we'll get her out of here."

"Looks like someone else'll be needing a hand, too,"

191

Mr. Sims indicated Mrs. Miller.

And then she spoke — the first sound we'd heard from her all afternoon. "But what *then?*" She turned her wild eyes toward Sylvie. "What'll you *do* with her?"

Nanna, stepping toward Mrs. Kyle in the back of the cellar, putting her hand on Mrs. Kyle's arm, said — in a voice so low I had to lean her way to hear — "Remember that blue batiste of mine? The one you took such a fancy to?"

Looking at Nanna like she suspected her of sneaking some of Mrs. Miller's medicine, Mrs. Kyle said, cautiously, "Yes?"

"Well . . . she's going to need tending to . . . besides, we don't *know* how far it's gone . . . . If you can take her in," Nanna stopped, glanced toward the stairs, saw the others were talking, went on, "and *see to her,* I'll shorten those sleeves and let out the waist — so it'll fit you."

I couldn't believe my ears. Though Nanna had it in her to be generous, all right — to people in need, the people had to be more than any *little* needful.

For her part, Mrs. Kyle was saying, "You can count on me — and I won't let no harm come to her, neither."

In a louder voice, following the others out, Nanna said, "Betty Jane'll take the dog; Mrs. Kyle here will take

Sylvie." Then, turning to Mr. Sims and Reverend Jenkins, she said,"If you can just get her over there . . . ."

So, risen from the fiery pit, we returned to the world we had left. A changed world, now. Up and down Tenth Street, the tops were gone from all the trees; porch furniture and tree limbs and window screens were scattered in the lawns, in the streets — and across the rooftops. Mrs. Miller's garage was strewn about like discarded lumber; the Turners' roof lay a-tilt in their front yard; while over our way, our fence and our chicken coop were — well, not scattered — just gone. Nowhere to be seen. The hens, upset but unhurt, were perched in a row on the coping of our front porch, complaining loudly.

Mr. Sims and Reverend Jenkins got Sylvie to Mrs. Kyle's house; Nanna and I — both of us holding tight to his leash — got a resisting Taddy to ours; and Mrs. Miller — with unsteady steps — wove her way to hers.

A few days later Sylvie and Taddy were once again passing our houses on their regular errands — Taddy, complacently eyeing the world from Sylvie's arms, Sylvie, muttering and frowning, her eyes on the sidewalk —

and as always, speaking to no one.

The Sunday following the storm, the title of Reverend Jenkins's sermon was "The Voice That Spoke in the Whirlwind." Though, of course, he didn't mention it in his sermon, he had put it about that the Lord, in the Whirlwind, had delivered Sylvie of her burden.

As for me, I never could decide between the Lord and Mrs. Kyle. But, judging from the hours Nanna spent altering her blue batiste to fit Mrs. Kyle, there was never any doubt in *her* mind.

DREAM
ROCKET

N THE LATE THIRTIES, every day at exactly 1:20 p.m., just about the time Mrs. Arnold's English class was warming up to the ecstasies of Conjugation and Declension, the northbound *Rock Island Rocket* would mourn its way into Dixter, Oklahoma. At the sound of its first low moan, from down south of town, by the refinery, our interest in the Uses of the Nominative Case — never hardy — would begin to wane.

The *Rocket* was a modern, streamlined diesel; while the old-fashioned, black steam engines looked and sounded perfectly at home clacking and snorting across our dusty plains and past our cotton gins and tin roofs, the gleaming, silver *Rocket* was a startling incongruity. Something from another world. Bringing its bright proof that out beyond our sea of dust lay a land where people like Greta Garbo and Joan Crawford moved among white pianos and satin-tufted chairs. (We knew exactly what that land looked like — we had seen it in the movies at the Palace Theatre down on Main Street.)

Sitting in class, listening, we could follow the *Rocket's* approach by counting off the crossings where it sounded its warnings. At first, just small bleats of complaint, faint and intermittent, becoming — by the time it reached the Civilian Construction Corps camp — a suppressed moan, soft and civil. Usually at this point, Millie Webster's preening fingers would pause on a careful curl. Then the cemetery crossing — loud, intrusive, insistent. Doris Hall's squinty eyes would give up trying to focus on the blackboard, settling relaxed on some point of private vision. Reaching the edge of town, where the crossings followed in fast succession — the cotton gin, the oil well cementing company, the lumber yard — it became one long sustained wail, like the unassuageable grief of some unearthly mother, keening for her young.

By this time, Al Miller was holding his pencil like a scalpel over an appendix; Happy Wilson's perennially grinning eyes would be studying his farm-stained fingernails; while Mrs. Arnold's enthusiasm for Parallelisms and Antitheses would slowly wane, her voice wavering and running down like our hand-wound panatropes, her

198

eyes filling with tears.

I had a special reason for believing the *Rocket's* promise of a better land: half a century earlier, Nanna, my grandmother, had found her way to *her* dream by stepping onto a northbound train. Not the sleek silver *Rocket*. Just a dirty hooting steam engine. And not that I thought much of her dream — coming to a place like Dixter.

Still, to give her her due, that was years and years before the Dust Bowl or the Depression.

In Millie Webster's eyes dreams sat well. Slight, blonde, smirking Millie, who never wore hand-me-downs or made-overs. In Doris Hall's squinty eyes they looked like sheer shiftiness. Doris wore twice-handed-down-made-overs — from Nanna to me and then to her (how the dresses made their way from my closet to hers, I never knew, but every fall and spring, Doris would appear in some of my last year's made-overs). As all these were the cast-off finery of our parents and aunts and uncles and grandparents, we made a pretty sight in our prairie schoolrooms, like children playing grown-up.

As for Happy Wilson's dreams . . . Dixter, we figured, was dream enough for him, coming in from the country like he did, with a good part of his father's dried-up farm still clinging to his pomaded hair, with his sharp-creased striped overalls and his heavily blued and starched white shirt.

Al Miller was different. He didn't have to dream: to him the future had announced itself — he was to be a great surgeon. Meanwhile, many a Dixter cat, out for a stroll, became the subject of non-elective surgery.

Mrs. Arnold's dreams? Of what use were dreams to her — a middle-aged woman (at least thirty-eight) with a penchant for the labyrinths of the paragraph?

The movies and Dixter were all that we knew. According to the newsreel pictures, the Dust Bowl was high drama — great drifts of sand, worthy of camels and of sheiks who looked like Rudolph Valentino. *Our* Dust Bowl was far less photogenic — a faded brown daguerrotype, smudgy and dim, the brown sky indistinguishable from the brown land.

At the same time that the Dust Bowl was shrivelling our grass and our corn, the Depression was shrivelling our souls. At home, our fathers sat silent and ashamed in the dark corners of our living rooms. At our back doors, strangers knocked, asking to do odd jobs in return for a sandwich, a glass of milk, and maybe a night in the garage. At school, our teachers, unpaid, taught in unheated classrooms, their coats and gloves white with chalk dust, while sitting at our desks in our coats and caps and scarves, we crossed and re-crossed our legs to keep them warm, pushed our pencils through the ever-settling grit, and grated our feet against the sandy floors — our teeth on edge.

For our parents and grandparents, who discerned God's punishing hand in every adversity, the Dust Bowl and Depression meant a new order of fear — of having been abandoned like ungrateful hitchhikers on some highway of cosmic disorder. For them, the order of nature had cracked.

But not for us. For us, Dixter was only an aberration; the normal world was the one the *Rocket* came from and went to. And it was as unlike Dixter as the *Rocket* was unlike the dirty hooting steam engines that pulled the freight cars through town. All of us were going there — some day.

That the *Rocket's* moan, like the Pied Piper's song, lured only the young, we took for granted — making no connection, for instance, between it and Mrs. Arnold's tears. These, like itchy noses and scratchy voices and chronic coughs, we attributed to the dust. In our myopic vision we couldn't see that teachers, paid or unpaid, might have cause to cry real tears. Not until Mrs. Arnold's tears dampened her enthusiasm for matters of syntax and style did we begin to take them seriously.

It was in these days that I also began to take seriously one of Nanna's stories about her early life — the one about the train trip. As a child on a sharecropper's farm in Texas, she had watched the railroad crews preparing the road bed for the tracks (the same tracks the *Rocket* now ran on) and had asked her father where the road would go and what kind of wagons would travel over it. Some day, she had promised herself, she would ride over that funny new road to a real town. If she lived in a town, she figured, she could earn enough money to buy a sewing machine. And with a sewing machine, she could become a seamstress. That was *her* dream.

When the very first train, spilling cinders through the open windows, pulled into Dixter in the 1890s, Nanna was on it. But not as she had imagined. Orphaned at fourteen, she had been sent by the Baptist country preacher to do the only thing orphaned girls could do — domestic work as live-in slaveys.

This was back before statehood, when Dixter was just a small trading settlement in Indian Territory, but it seemed a fine enough town to my grandmother stepping off the train, brushing away the cinders from her mother's washed-out market dress. (When the church ladies had come to lay her mother out, one had insisted on using the Sunday dress, "It's only fittin' she git laid out in somethin' decent." Another had held that "It's only decent the child should git sent off in somethin' fittin'." Decorum had won out over need.)

From the crunch of the gravelled trainbed she crossed over to a wooden sidewalk that clacked under her feet. "I thought I was entering Paradise," she said, recalling the day. "Walking on a sidewalk, thinking about shoes that had maybe never been baptized in mud and manure . . . ."

Walking up the main street she saw, besides just the usual harness shop and hardware store and dry goods store, a secondhand store with a *piano* in the window. Out from the main street a few other streets straggled off into the countryside; on one, a cotton gin so new its tin roof still glistened in the sun; on others, houses fresh with new paint. Last, she looked out toward the rise north of town, the highest piece of ground for miles around. There the city fathers, confident of the future, had built a water tower big enough to serve a county seat if statehood should come; that same tower, fifty years later, bore witness not just to the foresight of those city fathers but also to the once high spirits of our own fathers, with such testimonials as "Class of '11" or "Class of '17."

"Lord, lord," she reminisced, "it made me forget how scared I was."

In such a town, she felt convinced, lived ladies who wore hats to Missionary Society, who would pay other people to do their sewing for them.

Hearing that story was like having my fortune told: just as her cinder-snorting steam engine had brought her to Dixter, my diesel-powered *Rocket* would take me to some place like Kansas City or maybe even St. Paul.

I told Millie Webster and her court. Impressed, they widened their circle to include me. They were diagnosing Mrs. Arnold's tears.

"Two to one it's her fast-pants daughter," said Millie's lady-in-waiting.

"Daughter?" asked another.

"Eighteen — and living *alone*. In Tallisaw."

"I still say it's a man," insisted Millie.

"*Her?*" Romance and Mrs. Arnold?

"Delbert Moore," Millie declared, watching as the enormity and scandal of it warmed them.

"Jilted her."

"She's been going out with *him?*" Delbert Moore was a widower with a bald head and a fine big house.

"Out *where?*"

Exactly. Single or widowed teachers (a divorced teacher being a contradiction in terms) were expected to take a room with some respectable family or widow (Protestant), to eat at their table, to have callers (if at all) in their parlor, under their noses.

Mrs. Arnold was a widow. What kind of romance could she have — in her landlady's parlor?

Nanna, I decided, would know about such things. From her days as a live-in hired girl.

Not letting on about my reasons, I asked her questions, got her to talking. "Did they let you go to football games?"

"Football?" She looked at me like she couldn't believe what she saw. "I didn't even go to *school!*"

"When. . .?" I was going to ask how she managed to finish her education — assuming, of course, that *everyone* had.

"Last school I saw the insides of was down in Texas. Eighth grade."

My own grandmother. Nanna. True, she'd embarrassed

me plenty of times. But never because of ignorance. More because of putting on airs, like giving her name to sales clerks as *Mistress* Ella Kelso.

"Met a boy from the school," she went on. "He'd pass on his way to the schoolhouse when I was hanging out the wash."

On one of those washdays he asked whether he could come to call.

"Didn't know I was hired help. Thought I was just doing my early-morning chores." Hired help, she explained, weren't allowed "callers."

I could see it coming — and it did. She started going on about how lucky I was, and the more she said the more I wanted to hand it back to her, to ask her how she thought it was any different for me — us with two sitting rooms and not a one I could invite a friend to. But I couldn't say it, because her ways were never direct enough to get back at — *she* never forbade me having friends in, she would say. "Where?" I might say, because ever since Mother died two years earlier, the only rooms that Nanna kept heated in the winter were the kitchen, the bathroom, her bedroom, and mine. In the summer when she couldn't freeze my friends out *that* way, she froze them out another, like the time she asked Al

Miller, "Your daddy ever make those payments on his mortgage?"

I never spoke up. My generation was a cowed lot. Or maybe the times, being so bad, instilled in us some spark of sportsmanship. It wouldn't take more than a spark to realize there was no real sport in baiting teachers who were serving without pay or in rebelling against fathers already sitting whipped in their silent corners. We didn't even leave our mark on the water tower, as our testimonial that we had passed this way.

What we did do was more cowardly. Devious. Deadly. Though we meant no harm. And were never to know, for sure, that we brought on the final trouble. We would tell ourselves, in looking back, that we had never teased Mrs. Arnold, never mocked her, never made fun of her — not even behind her back. We merely invented her. Filled our idle moments embroidering lurid threads onto the colorless tapestry of her life. We so thoroughly refurbished it that in the end, as we sat listening to the *Rocket* make its way into town, crossing by crossing, we often found that, compared with our scarlet imaginings about Mrs. Arnold's past, our own daydreams were just washed-out pastels.

Then one day, walking into English class, we saw a

new teacher sitting at Mrs. Arnold's desk. A substitute, we supposed. The next day she was still there. And the next week. And the weeks after that. And she had never heard of Parallelisms and Antitheses.

We never saw Mrs. Arnold again. Whether she left voluntarily, we never knew. Where she went, we never heard. Nor did we, this time, invent explanations. Knowing that we, ourselves, may have been part of that explanation.

The first Nanna heard of it was at Adult Ladies Sunday School Class, which had been taught for several years by Mrs. Arnold (teachers were expected — though not actually *required* — to teach a class in Sunday School). Nanna, having been to one generation a hired girl, to another a seamstress, and to another the wife of an alcoholic harness-maker who struck it rich in oil, was not privy to the gossip of the church ladies; so when Mrs. Arnold missed the second Sunday, Nanna asked the ladies whether she was sick — and she got an earful.

Walking home with her after church — one of those blowing days when it seemed like all the topsoil from the entire state of Kansas was being dumped down on us — I could tell she was upset about something, the way she was bulling her way straight into the wind and the dirt, not turning her face, not blinking an eye. I supposed she'd had a run-in with someone.

After we came into the house, instead of going into her bedroom to take off her girdle and her good clothes, she just kept walking, her Sunday shoes clicking on the hardwood floors. I could hear her opening doors that had been closed since Mother died; coming out of my bedroom I saw her in the dining room, wiping the haze from a pane of the leaded glass doors of the oak china cabinet, running a finger through the thick dust of the built-in oak sideboard, leaving a furrow in its wake.

"That poor soul!" she exclaimed.

"Who?" I asked, going into the dining room.

"Never you mind!" she snapped.

Opening the French doors into the library, crossing over to the windows, she opened the heavy dust-dingy drapes. A beige cloud rose into the room. At the oak bookcases, she opened one of the glass doors; these bookcases were a mere branch of a whole forest of oak in our house — doors, floors, cabinets, and ceiling beams. When my grandfather built the house in the Twenties, after he made his money, he lined two whole rooms with bookcases — the books, like the china in the dining room sideboard, were protected by leaded glass doors.

For the most part the books had belonged to my mother and my grandfather: hers an ambitious assortment she had collected and studied, in the vain hope that they would some day be *her* northbound ticket; his the history books he had bought to educate himself, and to arm himself against what he called the churched-up history of the preachers. There was one book whose owner I could only guess at — a mystifying, terrifying tome (two inches thick, published in 1886) entitled *Self Abuse.*

The library also held the panatrope, with Mother's recordings of Caruso and Galli-Curci. And not least, the radio. For, aside from the *Rocket,* Dixter's radios, with their smooth, flowing curves and arches, were the only tangible sign that had made its way to us from the world we knew lay out there somewhere beyond our ocean of dust.

Nanna opened one of the doors, reached in, and picked out Willa Cather's *Shadows on the Rock,* a gift to Mother from Mrs. Arnold.

Shoving it back onto the shelf, off she went, clicking her way down the hall to her bedroom, declaring, "The shame of it! If she'd had a place of her own — for her and that daughter . . . ."

210

When she came out, she had changed into one of her home-sewn cotton dresses; around her head she'd tied a towel. "Drought or no drought," she announced, "we're going to clean house."

As Sundays, after church, were a transient's luckiest time — big Sunday dinners, people freshly pumped-up with guilt and charity, and not the least, the prohibition against labor on the Sabbath — little could Jim (the only name we were to know) have imagined, when he knocked at our back door that Sunday, what he was in for.

As a concession to the day, Nanna did confine the project, in the beginning, to the basement, where neighbors couldn't see us. But Monday, by the time I got home from school (and was told to change my clothes, tie up my head, and come out and help), it had spread out all over the side yard. She and Jim had taken out the throw rugs and smaller chairs and the big burgundy-and-gray-and-black mohair-plush cushions from the sofa and lounge chairs and were flailing away at them in a vindictive fury of sweeping and brushing and beating.

Then, with me there to help, we lugged out the sofa, the floor-to-ceiling, lined-and-innerlined drapes, and the fake Persian rug with the heavy black design in the border. Together, the three of us flung the rug across the clotheslines, and Jim set about "beatin' the tar out'n it," sneezing and blinking his eyes, chortling and swinging and swatting like he was after the Devil himself. Nanna and I, laughing, grabbed opposite ends of one of the big drapes and, lifting it, snapped it back and forth so hard it gave out great popping, whopping sounds, like some live thing that the breath had been knocked out of.

The dust, rising in great brown billows, seemed to be reshaping itself into those dark clouds that, all those months ago, first blotted out the blue from the sky.

"'At'll learn 'em," Jim yelled, "packin' their Kansas dirt down to us!"

Wednesday afternoon, when our exorcism was centered on the dining room, when we had carried everything but the table itself out to the side yard and Nanna and I were getting ready to beat the rug, she said to me, across the clothesline, *"Betty Jane . . ."*

I recognized the tone: it usually meant I was in for it.

"You have any part in those stories?"

"What stories?" I asked, scared.

"All those lies."

"What lies?" Black lies, enormous lies — I could tell from the look in her eyes.

212

"I'd hate you had it on your conscience," she said, and she pushed a broom into my hands, so hard she almost pushed me backward.

By Friday night our rites were finished — the rugs back on the floors, the drapes re-hung, the leaded-glass doors polished, and Jim, with a bag of biscuits and sausage cakes over his shoulder and with his week's wages pinned in his pocket, had long since headed off to the highway to hitch a ride — going north, of course.

After supper, instead of Nanna going to her room and me to mine, as we had been doing for the two years since Mother died, Nanna went into the library and lighted the fake logs in the fireplace. Seeing her, I followed, turned on the radio, and we sat in the plush chairs and listened to "Amos 'n' Andy" and Edwin C. Hill. In the middle of the Maurice Spitalny concert, she got up and went back to the kitchen; when she returned, she was carrying two big bowls of buttery popcorn. Tired and happy (and cleansed!) we sat there munching our corn, listening to "Death Valley Days."

Which is not to say she had been cast from a new die. Though emboldened to think so, the following week, when Al Miller was walking me home from school, I invited him in.

"What's this I hear about those cats?" she greeted him.

One change, though, was clean and final: she never went back to the Adult Ladies Sunday School Class. And seldom to church. Though she did still send money — "Wouldn't want to live in a town that didn't have a church."

At the same time she took care to instruct me, "If anything happens to me, if I'm real sick, don't you be letting that preacher in to do his praying over me."

At school, those of us who had so heartlessly and merrily woven into the pattern of Mrs. Arnold's life our own dark imaginings allowed ourselves but one further conjecture: "She must have taken the *southbound Rocket.*" The worst fate we could imagine. Because for us, there was only *one Rocket* — the northbound: only up north did the world resemble the movies; down south, we were sure, it looked just like Dixter — beige and brown and brittle. (The truth was that four *Rockets* a day came through Dixter — two going south, two north; but the other northbound train didn't come through until more than an hour after midnight, and, being so long after our curfew, it didn't, so far as we were concerned, even exist.)

In the spring, not long before graduation, a spring that brought no bloom to the land or Easter finery to the young, Nanna had a stroke. Lying there in the hospital with the guard rails on each side, she could do nothing but make foreign, gurgling sounds.

As the days passed into weeks and she still was unable to turn herself or feed herself or put a tongue to words, and as I was running short of ways to show attentiveness, it occurred to me one night, doing my homework there beside her bed in the hospital, to read aloud to her, as I had read to Mother in the days of her illness. Thumbing through my English Lit. book, I came across "Lycidas," "In Memoriam," "Intimations of Immortality," "Ballad of Dead Ladies," "Remember Me When I Am Gone Away," "The Last Words of Juggling Jerry" . . . all, without exception, full of death. Then I came across "The Lady of Shalott" . . . full of dreams. Yes. What had she now but dreams?

I began reading. Got only as far as "Willows whiten, aspens quiver," when Nanna began to thrash about in the bed, helpless but determined. Tongue-tied though she was, she could still find ways to express her displeasure.

215

Laying the book on the floor, I marvelled at how, even now, I was fearful of her wrath.

A tapping at the door — I looked up to see it opening a few inches, and then the face of Reverend Jenkins. Remembering Nanna's admonition not to let him pray over her, I realized I was caught between that wrath of hers and the wrath of God. Jumping up, I rushed to the door, stood blocking his way. "She's sleeping," I lied. He said he would come back. I knew I must prevent him. Then, without my willing them or even inventing them, the words came — not mine but Mrs. Arnold's, and not hers either, as she had taken pains to explain to a shocked Millie Webster who, you could see, intended to waste no time in reporting such heresy.

"My grandmother," I said, and then I used the words Mrs. Arnold had used, "is at peace with her God — and has nothing to say to yours."

I thanked him for coming, closed the door — and turned to face her.

She was nodding her head. Fiercely. Plagiarism or not, I had finally found favor in her eyes.

Her third week in the hospital, she suffered another stroke. Called from school, I was met by the doctor in the corridor outside her room. "A matter of hours," he said. "Twelve to twenty-four."

Even where we stood, out in the corridor, we could hear, through the heavy hospital door, her tortured breathing. As though the alien marauding dust were taking possession once and for all.

I opened the door and went in, not wanting to see whatever I had to see. Her eyes briefly acknowledged my presence, then again all the strength of her being was consumed with her struggle for air. Only once more would her eyes turn to me — when for a moment she would look, intently, at her hand and then at me and then again at her hand: true to herself to the last, she was trying to tell me I was to let no undertaker's flunky get her diamond ring.

So wracking, so fierce was her fight for air, I felt certain the doctor must be wrong: she could not conceivably last the hour. Not like this. What I had yet to learn was that God grants no coup de grace, that even the losing are not allowed to quit the field.

It went on all afternoon. Into the night. Sucking so hard for air, she had sucked her cheeks into hollows. Her fingers had turned blue; her nose, sharp; and her eyes had become the eyes of a stranger.

Midnight came and passed.

The struggle went on.

About one o'clock in the morning the long grating gasps stopped, changing to short shallow puffs. I looked a question at the nurse who had come to stay with me: she shook her head.

Relieved that her cruel losing battle was almost over, terrified of what these ineffectual little puffs would bring, I stepped to the bed, took one of her blue hands in mine
. . .

And then I heard it, for the first time ever — the late-night *Rocket*. Down south, far off. "The refinery," I thought, at once shocked that such a thought, at such a moment, should intrude itself.

At the next crossing, I told myself, I will shut it out. But it came again, a faint moan, from the cemetery road. Then the lumber yard, raw and naked. The more harrowing its cry became, the softer my grandmother's breathing. "Can it be," I wondered, appalled, "that I am to count out her last breaths to the crossings of the *Rocket?*"

One long inescapable wail as it entered the town, then silence as it stopped at the station.

In the silence, I listened for the sound of a little puff. She was still breathing. Whatever the *Rocket* mourned for, I thought gratefully, it was not for her.

I was suddenly and totally caught up in an irrational wish that the train be delayed at the station, thwarted in its journey. Concentrating all my force on this, I fixed in my mind's eye an image of the old wooden, gingerbreaded station and, beside it, the silver sliver of the train, unavoidably delayed.

At that station I then saw another train, the first one ever to stop there, a hissing, cinder-blowing train, and a girl of fourteen stepping onto the gravelled trainbed and onto a wooden sidewalk, taking in the main street with her eyes, looking up toward the hill out north, out at the new water tower.

I looked back at the woman in the hospital bed with the sharp nose and the gaping mouth and the unfamiliar eyes. She was still drawing those short, shallow, useless sips of air.

And the *Rocket* was still in the station.

But it did begin to move, and Nanna continued to breathe. Mourning its way past the football stadium, drowning the slight sounds I was listening for, on it went, keening its way north.

In the interval of silence just after the crossing at the water tower hill, Nanna gave a few last puffs — and then but one.

Of those in Mrs. Arnold's English class who did find their way to worlds beyond Dixter, Happy Wilson — with a change of overalls and underwear in a laundry bag — went out to the highway and hitchhiked his way to eventual fame in an industry as yet unborn: television; Al Miller boarded a Greyhound bus for college and, later, for medical school; Doris Hall — well, as no one missed her until years later, no one knew just how she left . . . . Of them all, not a one took his leave by the northbound *Rocket*.

Save only my grandmother, for whom Dixter had always been world enough.

SECOND BEST

ECURITY IS TIGHT. We are allowed no incoming or outgoing calls. No mail. And no messages. We eat together in a cafeteria-style dining room. We share shower rooms and bathrooms, sleep two to a room, on narrow metal beds. We comb our hair by the light of a twenty-five-watt light bulb over the mirror of each lavatory. We have with us no personal belongings other than our clothes.

Except for the hour before Lights Out, our days are completely regimented. Each morning, each afternoon, and each evening we are allowed to leave the building, in groups of two or three or four, to proceed to the day's rites. Before leaving, we are warned not to speak to anyone along the way, and not to accept messages — either written or spoken.

The atmosphere, of course, is tense; anxiety, rife. One

young woman has already collapsed, and though a doctor was sent for, security being what it is, she had to be sent away.

Yet, given the gravity of the proceedings, we regard none of these measures as excessive. Because what is at stake is our lives.

For this is Sorority Rush Week at the state university. That week of winnowing out. Of separating the wanted from the unwanted.

Every single one of us sequestered here in this dormitory (except Inez Robbins) believes absolutely that if we don't end up among The Chosen, The Elected of God, so to speak, we'll be relegated, all through college, to some sort of social limbo where from a wistful distance we will watch the sorority girls as they pass, in their long satin formals, on the way to fraternity dances with tall boys in white ties and tails — while we head drearily off for a Coke date in the Student Union, with hay-haired boys who wear white socks with their black shoes.

No wonder hysterics are running ahead of the common cold.

Most of us have spent the last weeks of the summer getting ready for these few crucial days. Not reading books or anything like some people do before going to college. Just getting our wardrobes collected — fall clothes, even though the daily temperature in the first week of September can be counted on to reach a hundred degrees. For Mildred Parsons, who is assigned to the same room with me, this has meant a summer of sewing. For Hortense Henthorne, a summer of shopping, of trips to Neiman-Marcus in Dallas.

Mildred is from a country town down in what we call the "mountains," the Kiamichi hills, to be more exact. With her naturally curly brown hair and her big round eyes with the long lashes that fade into blonde at the ends and that she doesn't know enough to darken with mascara, she would look best in simple dresses with round collars, like Janet Gaynor wears. Instead, she has spent the whole summer stitching up stuff that would challenge even Marlene Dietrich — like the turquoise suit topped with the red foxes her mother wore back in the Twenties: *two* red foxes, staring glass eyes and all.

After room assignment and an orientation talk from Mrs. Throgmorton, the dormitory hostess (already dubbed Mother Superior), after unpacking our bags and showering, we congregate up and down the halls and along the stairwells, all of us wearing our brand new robes. One look at these robes and I suspect the worst:

that Rush is just a formality — we were already graded and sorted, long before we got here. The robes fall into two categories. Fluffy-and-practical. And slick-and-sleek. (Mine is a fluffy chenille, good for many washings, guaranteed to make the wearer look lumpy and dumpy).

And then there is Hortense Henthorne's robe. In a class all by itself. Though exactly like all the others in the "sleek" category — tailored, belted, with piping on the lapels and pockets, like men's pajamas — *hers* is black satin. With white satin piping and with her initials monogrammed on the breast pocket. With her thick black hair and her black-red lipstick, she makes the rest of us look like we've been pieced together by maiden aunts.

While most of us cling together in small clusters of instant intimacy, like people on a lifeboat, Hortense — off to herself — leans against the wall beside the door to her room, smoking. Only in the security of our clusters do we dare approach her.

"God!" she greets us. "You ever seen such a dump?"

Anxious to appear like people who have, indeed, never seen such a dump, we curl our lips.

"If I don't get a bid from Deta Beta, I'm getting out of here." She reaches into her monogrammed pocket, pulls out a green package of Lucky Strikes and a gold lighter.

Humbled by her audacity and courage, we say nothing, just contemplate our own timidity and cowardice.

"All the others — nothing but a bunch of yokels," she declares.

And probably wear chenille robes, I think.

"What I'll do is, I'll call Daddy," (coming from those black-red lips, "Daddy" has a funny ring) "and have him take me to Miss Hackaway's." Miss Hackaway's is an expensive finishing school, down in Texas.

Dispirited, our little lifeboat moves on down the hall. Dropping back from the others, I whisper to Mildred, "I'm not even being considered by Deta Beta!"

"Me neither!" she looks around to be sure no one is within hearing distance and says, "And I'll tell you something else — I'm going to take any sorority that'll *have* me . . . Icky Poo or whatever."

"You, too?" I ask, and we snigger. (Her robe, of course, is fluffy-and-practical.)

Making our way up and down the hall, from one covey of girls to another, we learn that not everyone is so easily pleased. Though only a few go so far as Hortense — absolutely refusing to settle for Second Best — several say that if it comes down to Third Choice, they'll not go to college at all, but just head straight for secretarial school. Two of us, on the other hand, appear almost indifferent to these High Mysteries called Rush. Inez Robbins. And me.

Inez is engaged and is going to be married at the end of this first semester. So, in this business of choosing and being chosen, *she* has skipped a grade or two, jumped right over the sorority, the major, the minor, the job — right to the Finish Line.

And then me.

"You secretly pledged?" Hortense goes straight to the point.

Secret pledging, if tolerated, would short-circuit the whole system, like a football player sneaking out to the stadium the night before a game and running a few touchdowns — all alone — and then writing them down on the scoreboard.

"No!" I'm shocked, to be accused of such an offense.

"Then why're you so goddamned above-it-all?" she asks.

It's true. I *am* above the fray. And I do have a secret. Except that it's not a real secret, not something that must not be told. It's just something I don't know *how* to tell. It's too enormous and wonderful and frightening.

My secret — and I have told no one — is that I have found my father.

I lost him when I was four, when he and Mother were divorced. Since then (except when Mother and I visited him when I was five years old and he took me to the park and we rode the merry-go-round and he bought me a package of colored mints) I had never heard from him or of him. Then just before Rush a friend entering college back East found him for me, told him my mother was dead, told him my grandparents were dead. Together the two of them arranged for him to call me; "between six and seven o'clock," my friend wrote, "the first week of September," going on to say that on September 8 he was sailing for Singapore. Reading her letter, I remember Mother once saying that the very week after their wedding he had gone off to South America, looking for oil, and that he had come home so seldom and so briefly that he was always like a guest in the house.

As my friend knew I was leaving for the university, she told me to send her, immediately, a number where he could reach me. So I did.

The problem is *this* is the week he is to call. The very

week that not a one of us is allowed phone calls, or even messages. So, if I'm to get permission to take the call, I'll have to tell my secret to *someone*.

But now, knowing the someone is Mrs. Throgmorton, having watched her through our orientation session — so composed, in her flowered print dress, her single strand of pearls, her white hair in its immaculate French twist — having listened to her lady-like Southern accent spelling out the mumbo-jumbo of Rush rules as though they are God's plan for the universe, I lose heart.

I want her to be someone a bit fluffy and fluttery, someone who will say, "There, there, don't cry," who will understand, without me having to lay out before her, wound by wound, my entire case.

But she's not like that, and I *will* have to put it into words, enough of it anyway to present a plausible case as to why, just for me — someone she has never laid eyes on — she should stop the heavens in their courses.

So, standing in line for the ironing board (the last-minute push to get ready for tomorrow's round of parties) I try out, in my mind, one set of words and then another, turn them, reverse them, like pieces in a kaleidoscope, hoping each twist will yield up the magic combination. While Hortense Henthorne shares with us her infinite wisdom, "Forget morning parties — just for country cousins, who *have* to be invited to *something*," I try a matter-of-fact "My-father's-leaving-the-country" approach; while Hortense dismisses afternoon parties as "For back-ups — Second Choice," I tell myself that, Mrs. Throgmorton being what she seems to be, I should observe a certain fastidious distance, make it sound that my father (a father no different from others) is leaving the country on a long business trip and (quite naturally) wishes to talk with me before he leaves.

"The night parties," Hortense is saying, "*they* mean business — *First Choice.*"

Now, back in my room, rolling my hair in pin curls, getting a bit frantic as, still, I ferret through my mind for the right words, it occurs to me that perhaps there *are* no right words, no fitting or decent way to say, "I'm expecting a call from a father I've never heard from," that perhaps the fault lies not in *my* words but in the frailty of *all* words, freighted with so grave a burden.

Deciding this may be so, I abandon the effort, concentrate instead on the words I'll say to *him* — words in that other tongue, the language for speaking to a father.

Getting ourselves ready for the hot night (the temperature is ninety degrees), Mildred and I discover we have more in common than fluffy robes and a determination to pledge whatever sorority wants us. This discovery comes when, with the first warning blink, signaling that Lights Out is five minutes away, Mildred picks up her glass of water from the top of the chest of drawers, walks over to her bed, and proceeds to sprinkle the top sheet — just as though she were preparing to iron it — then, pulling it back, she sprinkles the bottom one; with both of them now nicely soppy, she plops herself down, looks up defensively and says, "Guess you think I'm crazy."

"I'll go you one better," I say. I pick up my glass of water, sprinkle both of my sheets, then turn the glass up and pour the remaining water down the neck of my pajamas, front and back.

As the lights go out, we lie in our cool, soggy beds, laughing.

"Betcha Hortense doesn't know these tricks," Mildred says.

"Probably spends *her* summers in Colorado, where it's cool."

Even so, I don't sleep well. Not because of what I have to ask Mrs. Throgmorton — I've settled on that. And not because of Rush starting in the morning. But because of the train whistle. The old-fashioned steam engine kind, with that lonesome, coming-across-the-prairie whistle, that coming-through-the-night sound.

Lying there listening to it, I feel like I'm being carried, right along with the train, through cities and across lands I saw years ago, when I was five years old and was on one of those trains, traveling with my mother, all the way from Oklahoma clear up to Maine. On our way to visit my father. Maybe to live with him again. Maybe, to call him "Daddy" again.

The trip went on, it seemed, for days and nights on end. Long enough, at least, that after we got there, when I was lying in the feather bed up in the second floor of his high steep-gabled house, I still had the feeling I was being rocked along through the night, and I almost expected to hear the train whistle telling me — as it had all through the long nights of the trip — that the train was taking me to my father.

The trip was long enough, too, for me to learn the pattern of its days, of dressing in the bouncing bathroom, washing my teeth in the doll-sized silver-looking basin, of breakfast on the stiffly starched white tablecloth in the dining car, the bright yellow calendulas in the silver bud vases, the shiny rows of silver all lined up at my place — as at Christmas dinner — and the bright-toothed smiles of the white-coated waiters.

Best of all were the long afternoons — playing cards with the wonderful-looking, wonderful-smelling man across the aisle from us in our Pullman car, the man with the dark skin and dark eyes, the thick hair with the tight little waves, and the beard that appeared, ever so gradually, between breakfast and dinner.

He must have done a lot of traveling on trains, for he came well-prepared — with books and cards and pencils and paper — and he didn't sit looking out the window, the way the others did who, thinking to be friendly, would invite me to sit and look out with them, while they pointed out to me what I could see perfectly well for myself. "See?" they'd say. "See the steeple? Over there . . . ."

In the mornings the dark man did his work, reading stacks of papers and writing on a tablet, and Mother told me I should just say "Good morning" and pass along to someone else. But after lunch he would say, "Sit down," and would motion to the seat opposite him. "Tell me what we passed this morning. I was busy, you see, and missed it all." Proud to be doing him a service, I'd sit down — slightly forward on the seat so that my legs (which were too short for it) wouldn't fly up, straight out in front of me. (This, of course, required that I sit the way the photographer taught me when Mother had my picture taken to send to my father — shoulders down, back straight, legs crossed at the ankles, the skirt of my dress spread out in a half circle.) Then I would tell him about all the marvels we had passed — a farmer out on his tractor, with the rain coming down hard all around him, and him dry, under a big umbrella that he didn't even have to hold because it was fastened somehow to the tractor; about the man fixing a flat on his car, and having to crawl under the car in the mud; about the wide rivers *with water in them* (in Oklahoma all the rivers I'd ever seen had fine red sand in them) . . . I was glad to have someone who understood such wonders.

Reaching for a tablet, he would then draw pictures of what I had described, and as he finished one, he would show it to me and ask, very seriously, "Something like this?" Always he would have added something to make me laugh — an angry face on the man working on the flat, as he looks down at the mud on his trousers; a windshield wiper hanging in mid-air in front of the farmer on the tractor.

After my briefing him, as he called it, he would ring for the porter, pull out from his leather case a deck of cards, and then, when the porter appeared — his mouth all full of bright teeth — my dark friend would say, very solemnly, "Would you please set up a table for me and this young lady?" And I would pull myself up very tall in the seat, trying to look like someone accustomed to being called a young lady, accustomed to having white-coated servants to do my bidding.

I would always know when the time had come for me to thank him and to excuse myself: he would add up the score, declare me the winner (and as I could neither read nor add, I never doubted his scoring), then hand me my prize, which was always the package of green mints served at the end of lunch.

One afternoon after the card games, after the time when Mother would say, "No more visiting," and would hand me the coloring book, we pulled into one of those stations where the porter would tell Mother, "Time 'nuf fer the young lady to take a stretch," would put out the step for us, and then with a slight bow hold out his hand to help us down.

Out on the platform Mother didn't say "No skipping" or "No running," the way she did in the aisles of the train, so while she went inside the station to buy Life Savers, I played hopscotch on an imaginary grid of lines.

When she got back on the train, she agreed to let me stay out a while longer, provided I stay where she could watch me from her window — and she indicated the baggage wagons at one side and the station doors at the other.

Through an open window of the station office I saw a man in a green visor — just like the one my grand-daddy had brought me once from Oklahoma City — and I went over to see what he was doing, bent over, looking so intently at whatever it was. Well, it wasn't much, I discovered, just a small machine that he kept poking at with one finger, that sounded something like a type-writer, but wasn't — I had seen a typewriter. Besides, nothing was happening on the paper in front of him.

As I turned away, I saw that the train was moving. But, being by now an old hand in the ways of trains, I thought nothing of it, thought it was just one of these move-a-few-feet motions I'd grown to know. Or one of those jerk-forward-and-then-jerk-back motions. But the train wasn't jerking, and it didn't stop, and it didn't slow down, and it didn't back up. It was just slowly, steadily, pulling away, picking up speed as it went.

I started toward it — saw it rolling past me.

I saw Mother's face, her mouth open — calling to me, calling words I couldn't hear, her hands spread out against the glass of the window — then she was gone . . . passed on beyond me, out of my sight . . . forever, I was sure.

I felt like I was falling off the world, into an upside-down sky, watching the world fly away from me.

I called out for the train to stop, started running after it, tripped over something but, trying to hold onto the train with my eyes, I didn't look down to see what it was, just got up and ran on. Past faces turning to stare, past arms reaching out to stop me, past a voice calling "Little girl . . ." Then the grosgrain ribbon bow on one of my shoes came untied, and I stumbled, hopped along, dragging it, lost it, and left it lying there.

Just as I thought I was catching up with the train, I realized it was slowing down. Stopping. Then backing, slowly, into the station again. And now I could see Mother, no longer at the window but in the vestibule where the porter had put the steps out. Behind her, his head looming over her shoulder, looking out at me, was my dark and lovely friend.

On it came. Passing me. I turned, started running back. Even before the train stopped, I saw him, saw my wonderful friend, there ahead of me, jumping from the high train, landing in a crouch, straightening up, running toward me, smiling, holding out his arms to me.

Not slowing down, I ran straight into those arms, felt them close around me, felt his whiskers against my face, the rough wool of his coat. The feel of that coat became the dimly remembered father I was returning to. And this was how it was going to be — the beard, the rough coat, the arms — this was what a father would feel like.

Each night, lying in my berth, I would look out at the black land going by under the silver sky, listen to the train whistling its news of where it was taking me. All through the night that sound would drift in and out of my dreams, becoming for me — then and forever — the sound of expectation.

While everyone else heads for the dining room for breakfast, I head for Mrs. Throgmorton's office, just hoping she's in a good mood at this time of day. I have no choice, because right after breakfast we file off for the first of our parties, then after the party file back to the dorm, take off our sweaty clothes and hang them to dry, put on a summer cotton and rush downstairs for lunch, rush back upstairs and change into fresh fall outfits . . . and so on, until the last party of the day ends at nine-thirty tonight. So, in case he calls this evening. . .

The door is open and Mrs. Throgmorton is in her office, wearing a print voile (a bluish one, this time), her French twist as carefully combed as last night, and sitting as straight as she was standing then. She doesn't see me here in the doorway.

In one hand she's holding out a spoonful of oatmeal, reaching it toward a middle-aged woman in a wheel-chair, a mouse-colored woman who is a dead-ringer for Zasu Pitts. Just holding it there, steady, while the head of the middle-aged woman bobs, up and down, back and forth, up and down, her mouth hanging open.

Oblivious of me, as patient as a fisherman watching a cork in the water, Mrs. Throgmorton watches. Waits. Spoon in hand.

With a quick, darting movement, the spoon disappears, reappears, empty.

Now, very calmly, with a slight air of resigned conde-scension, she turns to me. "Yes?" she says.

I am already having trouble enough with my little speech, without this. I've heard about a crippled daugh-ter — but I expected someone *young*, someone maybe with a limp or a shriveled arm. The truth is, I didn't expect to have to deal with the *fact* of her. And not like this, head-on. And most especially, not now.

"Well?" Mrs. Throgmorton looks at me briefly, turns back, dips up another spoonful of oatmeal.

I stammer my way through a few tidy, noncommittal facts, falter, as I watch another spoonful of oatmeal disappear.

Without so much as looking my way, she says, "The rules are quite clear. No calls — incoming or outgoing."

For the first time ever I have invoked that word: *father*. And the Red Sea has not parted. I try again.

Giving me a my-dear-don't-pull-that-one-on-me look, she says, "Parents, of course, are the most usual conduit." She doesn't understand. Not at all. And how can she? With me expecting this nice, well-laundered recital to speak for all the years that have brought me here to her doorway with this plea, for the months when Mother was ill, when I lay awake at night hoping *he* would come to us, for the nights after she died, when I put myself to sleep with the story about the alley light . . . . This light, though nothing but an oversized bulb in a battered metal reflector, forced me to keep my bedroom blinds drawn, winter and summer; and even then a few pencil-thin beams — sneaking in at the edges — would stripe my walls with ribbons of white light. One of these beams, slanting its way across to the dressing table, fell directly onto a cut-crystal perfume bottle that had belonged to Mother, and as it struck the sharp prisms of the bottle's surface, it would shatter, flying off into bright shards of purple and blue and red and orange, which would then hang, suspended, over the bottle — a bright, shimmering fan.

Lying there in the dark, my eyes fixed on the fan, I would tell myself that, just as those few drops of perfume remaining in that bottle were the distilled residue of flowers long dead, so were they also some unquenchable essence that was Mother, and that the bright fan, shining toward me across the dark room, came not from the ugly light in the alley, but from that essence — from *her.*

Believing this, I would fall asleep, forgetting about the father who would not come for me.

Of course, I tell Mrs. Throgmorton none of this. What I do tell her, this time, she seems to be listening to, for a while, though still she never looks at me, just keeps her eyes on that spoon and that mouth. When she starts putting away the breakfast — placing the spoon in the bowl, picking up the box of tissues she uses for wiping the daughter's mouth, stands, turns her back on me — I feel sure she is dismissing me.

242

I stop. Wait.

Still paying me no attention, she takes a step or two over to a spindly desk that looks like a relic salvaged from long-forgotten proprieties, from a time when ladies penned polite invitations. Her back still to me, she places the plate and the box of tissues on the desk.

Half frantic, half furious, I wait.

Turning, she says in that low, proper voice of hers, "My dear, some things are beyond the scope of *rules.*" Then she comes over to the doorway, where I'm still standing, places a hand on each of my shoulders, says, "Between six and seven o'clock, *nothing* will drag me away from this phone."

Then the surprising thing happens — though maybe I shouldn't be surprised: as I thank her, I notice that the daughter, in her shaky way, is looking at me, and that her eyes seem to tell me she understands.

I hadn't realized I was talking to *her* too.

I sit at the first table inside the dining room, where Mrs. Throgmorton can come to the door and nod to me when my call comes. Though I wish they wouldn't, Mildred, Hortense, and Inez join me. With my insides feeling like all my bones and muscles have dissolved, I pretend I'm not hungry. It proves easy enough, thanks to Hortense, sitting there making faces and saying, "Daddy feeds his hogs better slop than this!"

As the time draws closer and my fingers grow colder, I find myself thinking the whole idea of the call is crazy. What can either of us say to the other? I can hear it: "How have you been — all these years?" And will he ask, "Are you auburn-haired, like your mother?" And shall I ask, "Are you bald? Or fat?" Come to think of it — having gone so long without any father at all, I see no reason to settle for a fat one.

Hortense, running her fingers through her thick black hair, treating us to the sight of her long nails with the red-black polish that matches her lipstick, has started on her same old spiel, her "Deta Beta or I'll call Daddy" bit. Spoiled brat.

At first everyone admired her spunk, not just for refusing to settle for Second Best, but for *saying* it in advance, like getting out on a limb and handing someone a saw and then inviting your friends to come and watch. But more and more she's beginning to sound just plain pig-headed, like those pampered princesses in the fairy tales, with all the suitors in the land — and sometimes other lands as well. And what do they do? Announce that not a one of them is good enough, that thank you very much but they'll just hie themselves to a nunnery.

My thoughts must be reaching my face, because I hear Hortense saying, "Look at that smirk! Don't tell *me* she's not secretly pledged."

"Or maybe secretly engaged," says Inez, who goes around half the time smiling at her own thoughts — thinking about the wedding or the honeymoon or you-know-what.

I smile and say nothing. I'm listening for the sound of a phone.

Dinner comes at last to an end. The vigil is over — for tonight.

On the way back to my room, I go to Mrs. Throgmorton's doorway to thank her for staying by the phone, but seeing she's in stern conference with a rushee who was seen speaking to a fraternity boy as she returned from a party, I wave and go on past.

Returning to the dorm for lunch today, unfastening the necks and plackets of our hot dresses the minute we start up the stairs, Inez and I notice up ahead a whole swarm of buzzing, half-undressed girls outside the door to my room.

I hurry down the hall.

"She's all right now," someone says as I approach.

"Who?"

"Mildred. Heat-stroke."

Going into the room, I first see the red foxes, hanging across the foot of the bed, then Mildred, lying with her face turned toward the wall.

"Guess I'll have to drop out of Rush," she says, still not turning to look at me.

"Oh, no you won't!" She's looking for a way out, I'll bet anything. A face-saver. "You'll just quit suffocating yourself with *these.*" I pick up her two leering beasts, toss them to the other bed.

"Then what will I wear?" She turns now and looks at me. "I worked on that suit for weeks."

"You can *carry* the jacket, toss it over your shoulder as you go into the party."

"You think so?"

"I *know* so," I answer, directing a look of triumph into those beady glass eyes at the foot of the bed.

One of the unofficial rituals of Rush, I learn, is Running the Row. At five o'clock every day, when the afternoon parties end and all of us head back to the dorm, the fraternity boys line up like an honor guard on both sides of the sidewalk along Fraternity Row and, knowing perfectly well we are not allowed to speak, they hoot, jeer, whistle, turn somersaults — anything to bait us into a response. For the girls from the larger towns, who recognize hometown boys, it's the highlight of the day: they wink, roll their eyes, throw kisses; but girls from small towns, who know no one — like Mildred and me — we walk along with our heads lowered, our eyes on the ground, like nuns going up to take the sacrament.

Back in our rooms, Mildred is quiet. The parties, I'm afraid, are going badly for her. I'm quiet too, because it's almost dinnertime. Another vigil.

"How long until dinner?" I ask.

"Who cares?" she answers. "I don't feel like eating."

I say nothing.

Going to the closet, she pulls out a seersucker sunback (one of the few civilized customs of Rush is that in the dorm we wear summer clothes).

"Hortense is right," she says, "night parties are best."

She takes out a strapless green taffeta formal to press for tonight's party. "But she's wrong about *why.*"

"Then why?"

"The formals — they're cooler. Bare necks, bare arms, bare shoulders."

I grunt. I'm still making my way out of my afternoon dress — a black crepe with an accordion-pleated skirt, a long red chiffon scarf that hangs from the waist to the hem — and best of all, a high, black sequin collar. When I'm in it, I feel a match for Joan Bennett. But *getting* in it is another thing, with its complex systems of snaps, hooks and eyes, and zipper.

In this afternoon's heat, though, the beautiful sequins (where they turn under at my neck) have felt like the brass studs of a dog-training collar.

With everything finally unfastened, I lean over, lift the dress over my head, turn it inside out, and pull.

It hangs, catches — right at my neck. I pull harder. It holds fast.

Straightening up, letting the dress fall back down, right side to, around me, I feel the snaps (unfastened), feel the hooks and eyes (also unfastened); again I lean over, turn the dress wrong side out, and tug.

I call to Mildred, from inside the dress. "Grab the

front, will you?"

She pulls the front. I pull the back. The dress goes just so far and stops. At my neck.

"You sure you haven't missed a hook and eye?" she calls.

"Mmmmah!" Convinced I'm suffocating, I claw my way up for air.

Mildred starts a meticulous search for the hidden hook. "Jeepers!" she exclaims. "They're melted!"

"The hooks?" I'm impressed.

"The sequins."

I go to the mirror. She's right. My beautiful sequins, where they turn under, are now just a gooey black yoke.

Gingerly, with two fingers, I try to lift the collar. My skin lifts with it.

"What will I wear tomorrow?" I wail.

"*This,* if we don't get you out of it."

The first dinner bell sounds.

Once more I lean over, turn the dress over my head; she tugs. I feel the skin on my neck lift . . . . She gives a sharp jerk.

"No-o!" I yell.

"Did I rip the dress?" she calls.

"No. *Me.*"

249

"Creeps!"

Stifled, I pull the dress back down. My neck is burning, but I'm afraid to look in the mirror.

"Oh, dear — it *was* your skin," she says, adding quickly, "but just a patch."

Now I do go to the mirror. A raw strip the size of a half-smoked cigarette, with blood beginning to ooze out of it. And a good eleven inches of collar still to go. I have visions of going through life wearing high collars to hide my scar.

"You're lucky I can sew; I'll turn it into a scoop neck."

"Cut away the dress and leave me in the collar?" I can see myself, going to tonight's party in my low-neck pink velvet formal — with a necklace of black tar.

The second dinner bell sounds.

Like Cinderella hearing the clock strike, I rush toward the door.

Mildred, catching up with me in the hall as I slow down to snap and hook and zip, says, "Hey, fastened up, it doesn't show. You can wear it tonight, then after the party . . . ."

I'm not listening. I'm thinking only how out of breath I'll be if that call comes as soon as I reach the dining room.

250

For dinner table conversation, everyone snatches at my predicament like dogs at a bone. Won't they have a feast, I think, when I toss them the news that out of the nowhere, my father has called?

Another dinner hour ended, Mildred says as we leave the dining room, "Let's see if Mrs. Throgmorton has some sewing scissors."

I had forgotten all about the dress.

"I'll go." I want to thank her and don't want Mildred to hear. "You go on and dress for the party."

Sitting there, as straight as always, holding out a spoonful of broccoli to the bobbing head of her daughter, she doesn't see me. For the first time I notice the room, how small it is; looking across it, through a doorway on the left, I see the ends of twin beds, crammed together in a room even smaller than this one. This, then, must be where they live. And this office must double as their parlor — the old-fashioned word comes easily to mind, looking at the furnishings: a Victorian love seat upholstered with tufted velveteen, the straight chair she's sitting in, with its carved-oak frame, the spindly desk.

When the spoon disappears into that mouth and reappears, empty, I speak.

"Oh!" she turns, facing me. "You gave me a start."

I can see I did. Because both of them are crying.

"The flu, I'm afraid," she says, laying the spoon in the plate, pulling a tissue from the box.

As the daughter's eyes wobble in my direction, with something like recognition in them, I realize how rude I've been, ignoring her as though she were an inkwell. So I smile, nod.

"I don't believe I know your name?" I say.

"Dorothy," her mother replies.

"How do you do?"

"You must excuse us," Mrs. Throgmorton takes another Kleenex, wipes Dorothy's face, where the tears are now running down it. "It's just that whenever I get sick, Dorothy worries so, having no one but me, you see."

I do see. And from the way Dorothy is doing her best to fix her eyes on me, I think she knows — or hopes — that I might.

"Any scissors?" Mildred asks as I walk into the room.

"I forgot."

"Never mind. Hortense is going to *dissolve* them. With nail polish. Or Energine. Or make-up remover — she's got a whole drug store in that cosmetic case of hers."

252

"You know what?" Mildred asks as she sprinkles her bed.

"What?"

"I think they like me."

"Who?"

"Gamma Ramma," she's whispering, as though someone might be eavesdropping. Looking rather shamefaced, she adds, "I've been afraid maybe *none* of them would want me."

"You know something else?" I say. "I think Hortense is afraid too."

"*Her?*"

"It would make sense of all her carrying on. Her facesaver."

"Jeepers!"

I pour the water down my pajamas, turn off the lamp and, lying in the dark on the wet sheets, wait for the train.

The last of the parties is ended. Also the last of the dinner vigils. (No call.) It is night, and we are waiting for the bell that will tell us the sealed bids from the sororities have arrived in Mrs. Throgmorton's office. The hall is quiet. No gathering in clusters. No calling back and forth. We are in our rooms, packing our bags. Tomorrow we will move — to a sorority house, a dormitory, a secretarial college, Mrs. Hackaway's . . . .

The bell sounds. We emerge from our rooms, file silently down the stairs and into the lounge. One by one, as Mrs. Throgmorton calls our names, we go up and are handed a sealed envelope (everyone, she informed us earlier, will receive one, empty or not). Still silent, we go back upstairs, go into our rooms, close the doors.

Only then do we open the envelope that tells us who — if anyone — wants us.

Mildred, with a piece of paper in one hand, the envelope in the other, is crying.

"I got it!" she sighs with so much relief you'd think a doctor had just pronounced her curable, then catching herself, looks anxiously at me. "What about you?"

"Gamma Ramma."

She lets go with a squeal. In fact, the whole dorm is resounding with squeals. It sounds pretty silly, actually.

Doors are opening, the squeals spilling out into the hall. Opening our own, we go out. Such a lot of hugging, screeching, and rejoicing as you've never seen. Like long-lost kinfolk meeting up at the Pearly Gates.

I try not to look like a wet blanket.

In the middle of it all, Mildred asks, "Seen Hortense?"

We look up and down the hall. "Try the shower," Inez suggests. We go to the shower room, call. We go to her room. The door is closed. No light shows underneath. "Already in bed?" We look at each other.

Hardly anyone has bothered with breakfast. Everyone is still too giddy. Packed and ready to go, we're off to our different fates. Mildred and I, going to the same sorority house, walk downstairs together. In all the skittering about, we never did find Inez or Hortense.

As Mildred and I walk through the lounge toward the entrance, I ask her to wait, say I want to tell Mrs. Throgmorton good-bye.

"*Her?* Leave me out." With that she puts down her luggage and takes a chair.

I'm glad, of course.

But not for long. Not when I see that no one, *no one,* is stopping by. There the two of them sit, all alone, just as on every other morning or evening that I've seen them. Except that this time, instead of a spoon or a fork, Mrs.

Throgmorton is holding out a small glass of orange juice.

Absorbed as usual in her patient waiting, she doesn't know I'm standing here, in her open doorway.

As Dorothy's head wobbles my way, her eyes warm with recognition; she seems to be trying to keep me in her line of vision.

I smile at her; her eyes fill with tears.

Seeing the tears, Mrs. Throgmorton turns, sees me in the doorway.

"Oh, my dear," she exclaims, "we're so glad you've come. Dorothy's been anxious about you." Then adds, "I can tell, you know."

The tears I've not allowed myself begin to betray me. Having come in to say Thanks, I'm having to say Sorry, sorry, as the tears keep coming. I hear Mrs. Throgmorton saying, "There, there, my dear," see Dorothy become a wobbly blur, find myself wondering — out of the blue — whether with her there was ever any difference, say, between being young and being middle-aged and looking like Zasu Pitts . . . .

Mrs. Throgmorton brings me a tissue and I try again to say Thanks for those nights by the phone . . . when I hear behind me Mildred's voice. "Something wrong?"

Quickly, we finish our good-byes.

"Creeps!" Mildred says, looking at my red eyes, as we go back to the lounge for our bags. "Aren't you the one!"

Coming out into the eye-searing sunlight, I'm surprised to see the usually empty street filled with cars, with parents standing beside them, waving, yelling, and carrying on as though their own futures were at stake.

"What are *they* here for?" I ask Mildred.

"To help their daughters move."

"Two blocks?"

I'd not expected pledging to be a family affair. It does not improve my mood.

Rounding the corner at the end of the block we see, down toward the service alley behind the dorm, a big cream-colored car, a very fancy car for a service alley. Beside it stands a tall, dark-skinned man and a young woman with thick, black hair; she is pressing her face into the shoulder of a dark tweed suit.

For a moment I can almost feel on my own face the rough wool of his coat.

"It's Hortense," Mildred says. "And that Daddy she kept talking about."

"Yes," I say.

"Poor Hortense," she says.

"Yes," I say, "Poor Hortense."

257